STREETS OF GOLD

STREETS
of
GOLD

a novel by

MARIE RAPHAEL

A Karen and Michael Braziller Book

PERSEA BOOKS / NEW YORK

To Nana and Grandpa, Grospapa and Grosmama,
the ones who began the story

Persea Books, Inc., 171 Madison Avenue, New York, New York 10016

Library-in-Congress Cataloging-in-Publication Data

Raphael, Marie
    Streets of gold : a novel / by Marie Raphael.
        p. cm.
"A Karen and Michael Braziller book."
    Summary: Marisia, a Polish teenager, comes to America at the turn
of the twentieth century and must fend for herself on New York's Lower
East Side.
    ISBN 0-89255-256-5 (pbk. : alk. paper)
    [1. Emigration and immigration—Fiction. 2. Polish Americans—Fiction.
3. New York (N.Y.)—History—1898–1951—Fiction.] I. Title.

PZ7.R18122 St 2001
[Fic]—dc21   00-066892

Designed by Rita Lascaro
Typeset in Cochin

Manufactured in the United States of America

First printing

Acknowledgments

I owe a debt to the many writers and researchers who provided necessary background material for *Streets of Gold*. A primary source was *Island of Hope, Island of Tears* by David M. Brownstone, Irene M. Franck, and Douglass L. Brownstone. This text provided oral histories of actual immigrants which helped me create my own fictionalized ones. *A Pictorial History of Immigration* by Oscar Handlin and the Time-Life book, *This Fabulous Century: Sixty Years of American Life* inspired me through vivid, pictorial details. I also drew information from Irving Howe's *World of Our Fathers*, *A History of Women in America* by Carol Hymowitz and Michael Weissman, and *The Story of New York* by Susan E. Lyman.

In addition to exploring turn-of-the-century New York in books, I also made what seemed like on-site visitations to that time and place. At the Ellis Island Immigration Museum I literally followed in the footsteps of my own grandparents, who had once crowded with thousands of others into the baggage room, the Great Hall, the cafeteria, and the dormitory rooms. I listened to recordings of immigrants, studied their battered trunks and suitcases, the treasures they'd brought from home, and the life-size photographs that stared down on me from walls. I inspected medical instruments, immigration documents, ship registries, tags, shoes, hatboxes, gloves, tools, jewelry, and a melange of paraphernalia that made the world of the past come entirely alive.

The Lower East Side Tenement Museum, an 1863 tenement building at 97 Orchard Street, again brought my novel's setting into clear focus. Photographs, videos, historically accurate doll houses, documents, exhibits, and the building's own narrow corridors, uneven wooden flooring, and period lighting fixtures, bathroom, and decor worked their magic. Distinctly I could envision Stefan and Marisia as they strived to create a home of sorts in such a place. I could also picture them on the narrow, boisterous streets surrounding the museum — streets peopled by the thousands of current immigrants who today live out the recurring American dream.

The Tenement Museum and the museum at Ellis Island assisted my research in an entirely practical fashion, but, more importantly, brought me face to face with a distant, unacknowledged history. During my visits I was strongly moved by visions of my own ancestors. In such grim or puzzling surroundings, I realized, they were protected only by their own courage and hope, as well as by their vital sense of family connection. Those encounters with my ancestors continued to stimulate the writing of this book whenever energy or inspiration lagged.

I am much indebted to Anjali Browning and others at TreeHouse Books in California, which first brought out *Streets of Gold*.

I also want to thank my husband, Ray, and my sons, Nick and Neil. Through the writing of this book, they stood by me, as they inevitably do.

Streets of Gold

CHAPTER ONE

AS UNFORGETTABLE AS IT WOULD BECOME, the day the soldiers came seemed at the start like any other day. By the hearth, laid with a morning cooking fire that Papa had built, Stefan leaned back on a wooden chair. He tried to pull a boot over his left foot. "I can hardly get it on, Mama," he called out. "These boots, they're too tight."

Marisia dipped the breakfast bowls into a wooden basin of water and scrubbed bits of brown gruel from them with a bristle brush. The water was so hot it turned her hands red, as if it were slowly cooking them. Wavering steam passed across her face and made her blink. With a wet hand she pushed strands of dark blond hair back from her face.

"Your boots aren't even a year old," Mama told Stefan. She swept at the floor with a broom made of twigs. Clumps of dirt darted away, afraid of her. "We can't be buying another pair of boots so soon."

"Tell that to my feet, not to me." Stefan held his bare

foot up. Impatiently Mama tapped it out of her way. Her hair was drawn tightly back from her high, arched forehead. Watching her, Marisia still thought she had the forehead of a lady, although Mama had frowned the one time she'd told her that. "A lady!" she'd huffed, insulted by Marisia's compliment.

"Hit my foot again, Mama, if you want it to stop growing," Stefan teased, wiggling his toes at her. "You have to be firm with these feet if you don't want to buy any more boots for them." Mama swung the broom. When Stefan ducked his foot out of reach, she began to laugh.

It was just then Marisia heard, over Mama's laugh, the dogs' fierce, low-pitched barking as they crossed the yard, a pained yelp when one of them was kicked, and then their scurrying underneath the house. It was when Mama's laugh collapsed that their world collapsed, that life changed forever.

A man shouted. "That was Russian," Mama whispered. She moved with hurried steps to the small window that faced the yard, the broom trailing behind her. When Mama turned back, her face was white, all the blood drained away by fear. "It's soldiers," she said. "Stefan!" She pointed to the loft.

When Stefan took a step toward the ladder, footsteps sounded in the corridor just inside the front door. In a moment two soldiers burst into the room, their rifles pointed into the air. One soldier was tall; the other, short. The tall soldier stomped toward Stefan, roughly pushing Mama aside with the flat of his hand. Mama stumbled into the wall. Her gray eyes fluttered with fear.

Marisia took a sharp inward breath and gripped the bowl in her hand, its cracked edge stinging her palm. If the tall soldier touched Mama once more, she told herself, she'd hurl the bowl straight at his head. Her heart beat so loudly Marisia thought everyone in the room could hear. Drops of water fell from the chipped bowl onto her homespun linen skirt.

"You!" shouted the short soldier. Marisia's first wish was that Stefan had both boots on, because standing there with one foot bare, he looked as defenseless as a little boy.

"You!" the soldier yelled again as he moved toward her brother. "Stefan Bolinski, is it not?" The buttons on the soldier's uniform shone, reflecting a flame that shot up in the hearth from the dying fire. As he neared, Marisia could see the red scar that ran from his left ear to his mouth. It was as thin as a piece of thread. She stared at that and at the brown edges of his front teeth.

The short, scar-faced soldier's voice was hoarse. "You didn't appear for the army induction. You were called up in the lottery. You know the laws. If you're called up, if they pick your number, you come."

Marisia translated the Russian words for Mama, who had never learned Russian in spite of the czar's order that everyone in Poland must do so. "They're mad because Stefan didn't come for the induction."

"There's been a mistake. We wrote for a postponement." Mama spoke the words slowly and very loudly, as if in that way she could make the Russians understand her Polish.

"My mother says that we've asked in writing for a postponement," Marisia told the soldiers in Russian.

There was a clatter of boots. Suddenly Papa was in the low doorway to the room. His chestnut hair was rumpled and wild-looking, as wild as his eyes. He was breathing hard. Like Mama, he must have seen the soldiers when the dogs barked, and Marisia knew he would have run as fast as he could up the slope from the cow shed.

Behind his right leg, Katrina hid. With wide-open eyes she peered at the soldiers' guns. Trailing Katrina was the chicken with the broken wing that she'd made into a pet and that followed her everywhere. It circled Papa's legs. Over and over it clucked.

"What is it? What's the matter?" Papa asked in faltering Russian. Adam stood on Papa's right side, so close he touched Papa's elbow. In his thin fingers he nervously twirled a piece of straw around and around.

"Why didn't your son appear with the others? His name was on our lists. Trying to escape his duty, is he? That's an offense punishable by prison—by worse than that." The tall soldier said this. He tried to look stern and manly, but at Papa's angry scowl he lowered his eyes and his round cheeks flushed.

Papa said, "His brother died ten years ago in the czar's army. We gave one boy to the czar. That's enough. We need Stefan. We wrote and said that."

"You have another son." The short soldier with the scar pointed to Adam, who bit his lip the way he always did when he was frightened. The soldier's eyes narrowed. The eyes were slits in his hard face. "If you've one son at home, we get to take the other one."

At his feet Katrina's chicken attacked crumbs of bread, its eyes glittering with greed. When the scar-faced soldier kicked at it, the chicken flew into the air, feathers all aflutter, and Katrina gave a low cry. Papa put a comforting hand on her shoulder and said, "Adam's a child. Nine, that's all he is. He can't do a man's work."

"His age doesn't matter. You have two sons so we get one. That's what it says in the regulations, and that's the end of it," the scar-faced soldier said. He shoved Stefan on to the wooden chair. With the tip of his rifle he poked at the boot Stefan held. "Get it on."

Stefan bent to do so. The embers from the hearth glowed so brightly on his reddish hair that the tumbling strands looked as if they were burning.

"Don't take him," Mama pleaded, approaching the tall soldier, who stood to the side and shuffled his feet, embarrassed by her distress. "Somebody tell them it's a mistake," she said. "Marisia, say it in Russian! Make them understand. Aleksander died when they took him. Don't let them take Stefan."

"Mama," Stefan interrupted. "This begging of yours won't do any good."

Papa held onto the edge of the table to steady himself. His worried face was a farmer's face. It was as brown and furrowed as the fields themselves.

Behind Stefan's back, through the window, Marisia could see that the day was growing brighter. There were no signs of the cold, windswept clouds that had crossed the sky in the days before this one. In the village people would say that this was good weather for planting. Everywhere people would be telling each other that it was going to be a fine day.

A fine day! Not in this house. Not for this family.

When Marisia pressed her lips together, her full mouth flattened into an angry line. She tossed her head and, without thinking, stomped one foot. The tall soldier startled as she did and spun toward her. She held her square, stubborn chin up and looked right at him. Her blue eyes, which lightened in sunlight and glistened and teased and danced when she was in a good humor, darkened now. They were almost black.

Everyone told Marisia that she could never hide the way she felt. Her face would always give her away. Her cheeks would flush or her thick brows rumple in fury. Her eyes would glare and smolder, as they did now. The tall soldier saw that she was enraged and fidgeted nervously, straightening the cap on his head and brushing dirt off the sleeve of his jacket.

Agitated, Mama was moving about the room. "Stefan will need warm things." Into a large bag crocheted in strands of heavy twine, she hurriedly tossed the sweater Grandma had knit for him, a bar of soap, his two shirts, and his dark brown trousers.

"The nights are cold. The nights are still cold." Mama was talking to herself in a peculiar, jagged whisper, but suddenly she snapped words out so loudly, they made Marisia jump. "Help, Marisia! Food!"

From the screened cooler box below the floor Marisia

pulled out a round of cheese, a half-dozen carrots, and three apples. From the cupboard she took a heavy loaf of rye bread, the cabbage leaf that had kept it from sticking to the pan baked into its underside. She wrapped these foods in a clean rag and tucked them into the string bag Mama held up for her. Mama turned and poked Papa. "Sit, Jozef!" With one startled stare, Papa did as she ordered. "He must have your boots, Jozef. His are too tight."

"They can't take him," Papa replied. "It's too much." Katrina held the edge of Papa's trouser leg in her chubby hand. She gripped it tightly while staring at the soldiers. All the while Mama was drawing off Papa's boots.

"Now he belongs to the czar. You should be proud," the scar-faced soldier said. At the words, Katrina's chicken flapped and ruffled and clucked and Papa hissed.

"Proud of what?" he said. "I don't want my good Polish sons serving Russia's czar. He takes our sons. He taxes us to buy jewels and... What is the Russian word for carriages, Marisia?"

She gave it to him.

At once he stumbled on in Russian. "Carriages! Carriages and jewels! And in Poland people starve."

"You speak treason." The scar-faced soldier took a step toward Papa and swung at his head with the muzzle of his rifle.

"No!" Mama hollered. She pushed her hand straight at the descending weapon. The soldier's eyes were surprised, even frightened.

Stefan was on his feet. The scar-faced soldier turned

at his approach and swiped sideways. When the rifle hit Stefan's head, Stefan staggered back without making a sound, but Adam wailed loudly, as if he'd been hit himself. Stefan threw his long arms up over his head.

"Don't hit him," Marisia called as she took a step forward. Behind the soldier Stefan let his arms drop. Marisia saw that blood stained the sleeves of his shirt and matted his hair. Three red lines trickled down the side of his face.

"Leave my brother alone," she screamed, taking another step. At that the scar-faced soldier shoved his rifle against her chest and hurled Marisia backwards.

She stumbled to the floor. On all fours, body twisting, she looked up to see the soldier raise his rifle up again and strike Stefan a second blow that was harder than the first. Marisia pushed herself to her feet and lurched toward them. The chicken flew a foot off the ground, then skittered across the floor. It flapped its one good wing. It cackled wildly.

"Enough of this," the tall soldier cried out. "Let's just get him out of here." He caught Stefan by both arms and pushed him toward the door. "We don't want the boy dead. You can't make an army from dead men."

Mama pointed at drops of blood, the size of coins, that fell onto the floorboards. Terrified, Katrina scampered beneath the stairs, her chicken scurrying behind. There Katrina took cover behind the large, reed baskets where they stored the winter clothes and the yarns and cloth. Only the curly top of her head showed. In her arms, she held the chicken tightly.

Dragging the twine bag they'd packed, Mama ran down the path from the house, while Marisia followed at a trot with Papa's black boots in her arms. Behind them trailed the dogs. They barked off and on but kept a safe distance. The soldiers drove Stefan forward. Only when they reached the towering oak at the edge of their field did the soldiers stop. Stefan took the things his mother and sister held out to him. The side of his face was covered with blood.

The tall soldier faced Marisia. "Some would have shot you for what you did. Some would have shot your father. He'd better learn to hold his tongue."

Mama reached up with her apron to wipe at the blood on Stefan's left cheek. Her sleeves were rolled up. Her forearms were sinewy, as muscular as any man's. "I'm not really hurt, Mama," Stefan said to her. "These head wounds bleed clean. Don't worry. I've had worse."

Mama let the apron drop. "Papa's boots will be too big on you. Put a rag in the toe or they'll rub and you'll get blisters."

The tall soldier laughed. "We could have killed them all and here she is talking about blisters! These Poles are absolute fools."

"The bleeding's almost stopped, Mama. I'll be all right."

The scar-faced soldier pushed Stefan. "That's enough. Move!"

With one foot in a boot and the other bare, Stefan hobbled a step ahead of the soldiers along the road. "Good-bye, Mama," he yelled to her, turning back. As soon as he did, the tall soldier prodded him forward with the barrel of his rifle. One of the dogs, the tan male, howled twice.

The sun was gaining height in the sky. Light streamed into the oak branches over Marisia's head. Before many hours were gone, she thought, Stefan would be tramping in heat. She hoped that the soldiers would let him stop to put on Papa's boots. She hoped they would let him eat the food she'd wrapped. More than anything, she hoped Stefan would know that she wanted to take back the names she'd called him last night when he'd mocked a drawing she'd made, a drawing of Katrina as a princess. He'd called it ridiculous and snatched it from her. "I hate you. You're a stupid pig. I'll always hate you." That's what she'd told him.

Now Marisia called after him, "Last night, I didn't mean it! I didn't!" Stefan was far away, almost to the line of apple trees, and she doubted he could hear her.

Five months later Stefan came home. He'd deserted, he announced to them. The journey home had taken eight days. He'd hiked by night. By day he'd slept behind logs and in clumps of bushes where he wouldn't be seen. Sometimes he'd taken eggs from hen houses and eaten them raw or stolen into orchards for apples or found berries or eaten wild mushrooms. To survive he'd eaten anything and everything he could.

With his unkempt beard and long, scraggly hair, scratched nose, and torn clothes, Stefan no longer looked to Marisia like her brother. He looked like a common tramp—who just happened to have the same almond-shaped brown eyes as Stefan's and the same long, loose limbs, who liked to tip back on his stool like Stefan and whose laugh was a loud bark like his.

He told them story after story of what had happened to him. Only when Mama put food on the table did Stefan stop talking to gulp it down. He broke a potato apart with his fingers and hungrily devoured it. He forked noodles into his mouth. "Is there more, Mama?" When Mama reached across the table to take his empty plate, the light from the oil lamp flared in her excited face.

One story that Stefan told was about Papa's boots.

A Russian soldier in his unit had wanted them. The soldier said that if Stefan didn't give him the boots, he would tell the authorities that Stefan stole money and food or had tried to run away or planned to poison an officer. Then Stefan would surely be imprisoned or even shot. Didn't Stefan realize that the commander would take the word of a Russian soldier over that of a Pole?

When Stefan refused to give up the boots, the soldier hit him again and again, methodically, Stefan said, like a man chopping wood. Stefan fought back, but the Russian was twice Stefan's size. Finally, dizzy from the man's blows, Stefan quit. His ears were ringing and blood poured from his nose.

The soldier took Stefan's boots. He marched about in them while emitting piglike grunts of satisfaction. Eyes swollen completely shut, bruised, panting in rage, Stefan lay in his blankets at the edge of the tent and watched this. Laughing, the soldier picked up his own torn boots and threw them one at a time at Stefan's head. Stefan swore he'd rather go barefoot than take them.

Within a week Stefan's bare feet were raw. One night a Russian soldier, an older man, brought a pan of warm water into Stefan's tent. He bathed Stefan's feet, fretting over every particle of dirt. He said Stefan could get gangrene infection. It could be bad. He'd seen men who'd had to have their feet chopped off in order to stop gangrene from spreading into the leg. Carefully he applied bandages. Then he brought out the soldier's boots that Stefan had rejected. He begged Stefan to take care of his feet and wear them.

At this point, Stefan said to Mama and Papa and Marisia, he'd had two choices. He could keep his pride and let his feet blister and bleed as they were doing, or he could swallow his pride and take care of his feet.

"The most important lesson I learned in the army, " he laughed, "you know what it was? I learned to pay more attention to my feet than my pride. I took those boots, and I'm not crippled. I'm not dead." He wiped milk from his mouth with the back of his hand.

Adam moved onto his lap and tapped a drumbeat on Stefan's knee with a spoon. "Besides," Stefan added, bouncing Adam to the beat, "Russian or not, the fellow was a friend. How could I say no to him?"

Stefan told them how he'd performed drills and maneuvers. He'd learned to fire the rifle the army issued him and to stab with the bayonet. He could remain on guard duty for hours at a time in driving rains outside the tents of the officers or march all night without complaint. He could answer in Russian to commands. He could salute neatly. But at no time, he told them, did anyone succeed in teaching him loyalty to an army that wasn't Polish.

"Of course," Papa said, leaning toward Stefan. "This is what I've been saying all along. Salute the czar's soldiers if you have to. Bow if you have to. But in your heart, never bow to them. Never."

"You must not start him talking like you talk, Jozef. They shot a boy in Warsaw as a traitor last week for talking like this." Mama's gray eyes widened, and she rubbed a hand across the reddened, weathered skin of her face. Her hair was weathered, too, into a dusky brown. She pushed a strand that had fallen from the braid which circled her head back into place again.

There were dark circles under Stefan's eyes. "Oh, Mama! Look, I'm here. I'm safe. Don't worry anymore."

"Surely they'll shoot you for desertion if anyone turns you in, maybe that baker's son I never trusted. Eyes like the eyes of a fox. Always grabbing at my money when I hand it over the counter, that one." Mama's fierce, oval face tilted to the side. "You must hide very carefully, Stefan. You must promise." Her fingers tugged at the sleeve of his shirt.

"Yes, of course I'll be careful, Mama." Tired, Stefan slumped back into his chair.

Still Mama kept her hold on Stefan. She looked from one of them to the other. Her eyes were bright as glass. "They'll kill him if they find him here. We will tell no one — no one, do you hear me?"

Stefan hid. Only after dark did he join them in the house. At the first sign of light he retreated again to the small loft in the cowshed. There he spent all the sharply colored days of autumn. Wrapped in blankets to stay warm, he was there when the first snows came.

He rarely complained, but once, while Marisia sat with him, he stared out at birds that settled on the highest branch of a barren oak tree. As if at a signal, they flew up in a small, flickering cloud. "I'm bored in here. It's like a prison," he announced. He watched the birds spin into the sky. Marisia put a hand on his arm and watched the birds with him.

It was Papa who spoke up finally against the hiding. "Stefan's a man now. He can't hide in a pile of hay forever." Papa twisted and pulled angrily at his bristly mustache as if he wanted to pull it right off.

And from that day onward Papa began to talk of America.

He asked relatives for money. He said they could sell off the Bolinski land after the family had safely crossed the border and get their money back. He told them that in the end they could all come to America if they wanted. He and Mama would be there to welcome them.

In America, Papa boasted, life would be better. There would be schools like none in the village. There would be newspapers and books and gold coins and plenty of food to eat and meat every day of the week, not just on Sundays.

The night before Marisia's family left for America all of the relatives came. They brought presents — a scarf, a bracelet, a candle smelling of holly, a strip of woven wool, a loaf of dark bread for the journey, some hard, dry sausages. Marisia's grandmother gave her two pens that made firm, rich lines, a set of fine colored pencils in a tin box, and a dozen brushes.

"These were your grandfather's, all of these things. The brushes were his favorite ones." Grandma leaned very close to Marisia. Her eyes were wide like Mama's and sea-gray, kind like Mama's, worried like Mama's. The skin of her face seemed to be made of thin, wrinkled paper.

"You've seen your grandfather's picture of the river otter, his picture of your mother. Every day he'd draw. Always he'd find a little time. People laughed at him for that. Your grandfather didn't care what anyone said."

Marisia watched Grandma's compact fingers wrap around her own and saw that her hands were like Grandma's with solid knuckles and strong lines running through the palms.

"He would see something. He'd see sunlight in a tree. Before you knew it, there it would be, that same sunlight, right there on your grandfather's paper. You have his gift, Marisia. I hear people tell you not to waste your time with drawing. It's just what people were always telling him."

Grandma winked as if to say they shared a secret. She deposited the pens, pencils, and brushes in Marisia's lap, then left Marisia and went to help Mama set out food.

After dinner Marisia sat by the fire and took her baby cousin onto her lap. She would miss all her cousins — seventeen of them — but especially this baby Anna. She'd miss her best friend Elsa, too, and the wild stream where they waded in the summer. She'd miss the ornery cow that shifted and fussed when milked and that was now sold off. She'd miss the broad oak tree under which she sat to sketch whenever she could and this room, crossed by twisting light from the oil lamps. She'd been born in this room, in a bed pushed close to the hearth for warmth. She'd lived for thirteen years in this house — no, fourteen years really, because the day of her birth was only a few days away.

On the floor, Katrina's chicken scurried about, busy with all the crumbs that landed there. It dodged passing feet. It was happier at this party than it had ever been in its entire life, Marisia supposed. When the bird fluttered past Mama, Mama scooped it up to toss it outside, the way she usually did. This time Katrina screeched out. She sounded like a chicken herself. Desperately she pulled at Mama's skirt until, with a little nod of assent and a laugh, Mama put the chicken in her arms.

Sitting on a stool by the loom, Katrina gave her pet kiss after kiss after kiss on the top of its dusty head. Its beady eyes flickered. It ruffled its wings and tried to escape, its mind—what little mind it had—entirely on food. Katrina wouldn't let go. She clasped it tighter. In little gasps she began to cry.

Stefan crossed the room to kneel by Katrina. Behind his kneeling figure was a wall of logs, its chinks filled with moss that kept cold air from seeping into the room. Stefan's shadow appeared on that wall. It curled as he bent toward Katrina. Watching them, Marisia brushed her lips across baby Anna's fuzzy head. With her finger she stroked the baby's cheek. *Never again.* Over and over the words repeated themselves in her mind. *Never again. Never again.*

CHAPTER TWO

IN SECRET, HOURS BEFORE SUNRISE, Marisia's family climbed into a cart drawn by an old black horse who seemed only half-awake. The cart's large wheels turned, and beneath Marisia's feet the floorboards shuddered. She could just make out the dark shadows of all they were leaving behind—the thatched roofs of the houses in the village, a windmill in the fields beyond, the cross atop the small church. In front of the church was a pillar with a niche cut into it where the priest had set a statue of the Virgin Mary. As they passed it, Mama crossed herself.

The cart rolled along beside a stream. In the afternoon, Marisia knew, the village women would come there to wash clothes, their hands turning blue in the cold water. The cart passed the straight beech trees that lined the road. All was hushed, as if Mama had told the wind and the trees and the birds and the cicadas to be still, just as she'd told the children to be still.

By dawn Lutrek was miles behind.

All day they rode. With every hour the bench grew harder. Marisia shifted her weight to her right hip and stretched her legs out — colt's legs, Mama called them. Her friend Elsa said they were dancer's legs and that Marisia could one day be a ballerina if she chose. Whether they were colt's legs or ballerina's legs, they felt as if someone had tied dozens of little knots in them. Even when Marisia jiggled those legs, the knots wouldn't come undone.

"By nightfall," Papa called back to them from the front seat he shared with the driver, "we'll be near the border."

Marisia shifted Katrina, who slept against her side, onto her lap. On Katrina's feet were sandals made of birch bark. The toes of her feet were grimy with dirt. Marisia drew her fingers through tangles of the child's brown hair. In her sleep Katrina coughed. There were beads of sweat above her lip.

"What will happen at the border?" Marisia asked. Because the groaning noise of the wheels drowned out the question, Papa didn't hear her or turn to answer.

Stefan tipped back and forth and made a face at her. "Don't ask him. Don't bother Papa."

"What do you mean, 'Don't ask'? Why not?"

"She always wants to know everything," Adam said.

"You stay out of it, Adam. You always take Stefan's side, don't you? You're nothing but a copycat." To her satisfaction, Adam blinked and jerked his head back as if stung.

"Tell me," Marisia persisted.

Stefan only slapped the dust from his pants, ignoring her.

She glared at him. "Tell me!"

"Oh, all right. Just be quiet! We don't have permits to leave Poland and cross the border into Germany. Papa told me not to say anything about it to the rest of you."

"If we don't have permits, they won't let us go!"

"This driver's helped people who don't have permits before, lots of times Papa says. He'll get us across the border somehow."

As the cart rocked across a string of ruts in the road, Marisia held tightly to the side. How could Papa entrust their lives to an old man like the driver? She watched him scratch tiredly at his knee through a hole in his trousers. The skin on the back of his neck was loose and creased, and his ears stuck out from his head. Twice he flicked the reins over the horse's back with crooked fingers, but the horse didn't pick up speed. Probably he couldn't. Legs like sticks the animal had, and bones that jostled when he moved, and a moldy tint to his coat. He didn't look as if he'd run for years. What would happen if the Russian soldiers chased them?

Just after sundown the cart turned off the road and into a drive. In front of a weathered farmhouse a man waited. He was the tallest man that Marisia had ever seen. "Into the barn," he called. "Into the barn."

"I know," the driver replied in his scratchy voice. "It's not the first time, is it? You think I don't know to get out of sight?"

"Well, be quick about it or it could mean trouble."

The cart clattered across the wooden planks of the floor and stopped. Papa climbed down and caught Adam when he jumped, his arms outstretched. They stood for a moment side by side, Papa's arm around Adam's shoulders. With his wiry build and tousled, chestnut hair, pointed nose, and narrow face, Adam was a small replica of Papa.

Arching her back to stretch, Marisia watched the dark swallows zoom through the rafters. "Are we staying here, Papa?"

"Just for the night," Papa told her. "Help us unload the quilts now. We'll make piles of hay for our beds, and then we'll lay the quilts on them."

Absentmindedly Mama passed her hand across Katrina's head. Katrina ducked away from her and began to twirl around and around to make herself dizzy while Mama shook out a folded quilt, ballooning it in the air. "When I was a little girl my cousins would visit. There'd be a half dozen of them—sometimes a dozen. We'd jump off rafters into the hay. We'd make beds in the barn just like this and spend half the night talking. We just couldn't bother with sleep." Mama's face filled with the pleasure she had known many years ago.

Marisia thought that if Mama was enjoying it here, then it couldn't be all that dangerous. She went to the door and for a moment looked out over the still fields. In the last light of the day, they seemed as faded as old clothes that had been washed again and again and again.

A hawk swooped into the tilting light. Adam ran by Marisia to go outside, brushing against her.

Quickly, urgently, Mama called him in. "Stay by the door," she commanded Marisia in a tight voice. "Make sure the little ones don't go out. We must stay hidden, absolutely hidden."

"Yes, Mama." It wasn't safe, not at all. Fear, like a hand, caught at the inside of Marisia's stomach. Overhead the hawk cried out.

"It's time." Papa shook Marisia by the shoulder to wake her. In the window over her head, she could see the stars tossed across the sky.

"But it's still night, Papa."

"We're going to cross at night," Papa said. "We have to. They'd never grant us permits to leave the country, not when Stefan's deserted. Besides, permits are expensive. If they weren't, half of Poland would leave. Who would stay when Russia's czar's in charge of us? Huh? Tell me that."

"Nobody, Papa," Marisia said sleepily, giving Papa the answer he wanted to hear. As if Marisia were still a child, he brushed the hair from her face with his callused hands. His thick jacket carried familiar odors of hay and wood smoke. Marisia pressed her fingers into it. "What if we get caught, Papa? Will they shoot us?"

"No, of course not."

"But they do shoot people, Papa—the czar's soldiers do. You said that yourself."

"There's no reason to be so afraid, Marisia. This cart

driver knows the way. He's taken people over before. Within an hour we'll cross the border into Germany where we'll be safe." Papa lifted Marisia's square chin up and looked at her before continuing in his calm, drowsy voice. This was the voice that he used when he harnessed the mare or that he used to calm the dogs when he took out porcupine quills, the voice he used when milking the cow to keep her from kicking.

"The driver will take us to a town just on the other side of the border. There we'll board a train to Hamburg. It goes at flying speeds, faster than the fastest of all carriages," he said. Marisia tried to picture a train, but she couldn't imagine what one would be like. "In Hamburg there will be ships for America. And in America we'll be free. Then you'll be glad that we took this chance," Papa went on. "The next hour will seem strange, but after that, it's done. Come now. Get up."

Just as Papa had predicted, the next hour was strange. The driver loaded half a dozen wine barrels onto a farm wagon. He slapped at the one in the middle and turned to Stefan. "This one's empty. This is the one you'll hide in, young man. We must hide you well. If it's you they get their hands on, they'll shoot you. And they'll shoot me." He winked and cackled. "Can't have all that. It's too dangerous, shooting is."

Next the old man told them to sit inside the circle of barrels. "If you hear me talking with anyone, huddle down low and cover the children." In the knuckles of his fingers were short lines of dirt. When he pinched

Katrina's cheek, she slid away from him and braced herself against Marisia's shoulder.

The driver began to fork the hay over them. "I don't want to be covered with hay. I don't like hay!" Katrina cried out.

Mama made a shushing noise.

Her eyes shut tight, Marisia pinched her nose to keep from sneezing. With a jolt, the wagon started out of the barn. For what seemed like an endless time, it bumped along the road. Once Katrina whimpered and Marisia longed to say something to her, but couldn't.

Now the wagon shook so roughly that Marisia realized they were no longer on the main road. Tilting, the wagon descended a sharp slope. Marisia heard in the next moment the sound of running water. It would be the river they had to cross before the border, she realized. When they did cross, the wagon pitched from side to side, its wheels sliding across rocks on the river bottom. On the opposite side, the driver called to the horse, urging him up the bank.

As soon as the wagon reached the top of the rise and the ground flattened out, the wagon stopped. At the end of a minute, it started up again, but it only moved a few yards before halting once more.

The shriveled old driver would be peering through the darkness for any sign of the Russian border patrols, Marisia guessed. She listened with all her might, scarcely breathing. She wished that there were someone at the reins now like Karl, the neighbor's twenty-six year old son, who could wrestle a bull to the ground.

The wagon crawled forward. Why didn't the driver lash the old black horse and whirl them away to safety?

The stillness broke suddenly. "Halt," someone hollered. "What have we got here?"

"Hay and things for market. I've got eggs, fifteen dozen eggs. Honey and milk, cheese, sausage, things to sell," the driver called.

"Hand down your papers. Why are you out and it's not even light yet? What have you got to hide?"

The driver sighed loudly. "I need to deliver this hay to Heinrich Schleffer on the other side of the town before I return to market to sell my things. If I wait past dawn to cross the border, I'll be late. If you're late to market, what's left? The space in the back where nobody sees you, that's what."

"Your papers are in order. That's all right. Now hand down that pitchfork, and I'll take a poke through this hay of yours," the guard said gruffly.

The driver answered in a grumbling voice. "Nobody bothers me when I cross. They all know me. They know I'm too old for trouble."

"Do like I say!" The Russian's voice sharpened. "You got anything to hide, I'll find it. Give me the pitchfork!"

"Well, take your pitchfork then. Poke it with all your might. Waste my time. Waste your time."

"Jews, is it? Jews who shouldn't be going anywhere? Or some bloody Pole without a permit who's in trouble back in your village?" With a heave the soldier drove the pitchfork toward the center of the stack.

Marisia made herself as small as she could. She bent

over Katrina. The soldier grunted as he shoved the pitchfork into the hay again. Mama's nails bit into Marisia's leg. Marisia froze. Was Mama hit?

"Poke harder," she heard the driver calling. "I have dozens of Poles in there. Don't slack off. Get them." He now was laughing in wispy hoots. "I've got more Poles than eggs in there. More Poles than eggs, do you hear?"

Then the soldier was prodding the hay all along the circumference of the stack, but only half-heartedly. "What's this under the hay? This barrel here."

"Only wine. Not of the best quality," the driver whimpered. "It wasn't such a good year last year. Not at all."

"Not Poles, but wine, is it?"

"Don't take my wine." The driver's voice rose in a wavering cry. "I need to sell it! I have little money."

"Help me down with some of your good wine or those old bones of yours, I'll break a few of them. One casket is all I'm going to take. Stop your sniveling." A barrel thudded to the ground.

The wagon moved forward.

By a spring in the woods Papa bathed the small drops of blood from Mama's back while she held a blanket over herself. "It's nothing," she insisted. "He barely touched me."

Katrina placed her hand on top of Papa's and pushed at the rag. "Me, too," she said. "I'm going to fix Mama too."

Hunched up on a log, Stefan watched them. Beside him sat the driver, who nervously rubbed his fingers back and forth on his thigh. "I'm sorry he got you with that pitchfork. I couldn't stop him."

"As if it were your fault," Mama answered. "If it hadn't been for you, we might all be dead."

Papa broke into a shrill voice, an imitation of the driver's. "Poke harder. I've got dozens of Poles in there. I've got more Poles than eggs." When he laughed, so did Adam. Looking at the driver, he slapped at his leg in an imitation of Papa too.

The driver bent over a small fire to adjust the kettle of water and toss in a measure of tea. He drew three cracked cups from his pack. "The last time I crossed, I changed myself into a woman, and I had my 'niece' in a carriage. I made my niece holler for all he was worth when two soldiers stopped us. Told them she was having a baby any minute and said they were going to have to deliver it for us. That made them run!"

The driver straightened his crooked back. His laugh sounded like gurgling. "That niece of mine could have scared off a battalion of soldiers with all his yelling."

Papa said, "You're the one who saved us just now. I'd say you're the hero of the day."

It would be easier to think the driver a hero, Marisia thought, if he didn't wear dirty sheepskin trousers and if his front teeth weren't so horribly stained. Wind blew his hair into wisps. Pouring out the tea into his old cups, he was like no hero she'd ever imagined.

In the streets, the people of Hamburg pushed and pressed — hundreds of them, more people than Marisia had seen in her entire life. Over her head, on the third floor of a building, a woman flapped a wet sheet that sent spray flying on the passersby below. Bumped by a fat man who swore in German, Adam stumbled into Katrina. She started to cry. Just then a carriage passed.

In it sat a lady more beautiful than any person Marisia had ever seen. Cool and serene, the lady's eyes took Marisia's family in without a flicker and then swept past them to look with the same undisturbed glance at others in the pulsing crowd. Her blue velvet cape was the same color as the deep spring in which Adam had caught a giant trout last summer.

Seeing Marisia look so intently at this lady in the blue cape, Mama wheezed, "That woman doesn't look as if she's put in a day's work in her life."

"But she's like a queen," Marisia argued.

"A queen's no use to us. Fairies, queens, knights in armor—this girl's head is always full of nonsense!" Mama was announcing this to anyone on the street who wanted to listen, turning her head from one pedestrian to another. Marisia wanted to shout at her to stop.

"There," Papa called out. "There's the place." He pointed to an inn where someone on the train had told them they should stay.

An old woman led them up three flights of winding stairs to a cramped room. Papa's head almost touched the ceiling. Papa pushed aside a candle in a holder that stood on a small, scrubbed table so Mama could put out food. Hungrily they fell upon the cheese, cucumber pickles, and sausage, and the piroshki Grandma had made, which were filled with wild mushrooms from the forest outside the village. Papa said, "We're lucky our boat leaves tomorrow. Some people have to wait for weeks. They spend half their savings on a room like this before they even start for America."

That night Mama and Papa and Katrina slept in the bed, while Stefan, Adam, and Marisia spread quilts on the floor. From her own quilt Marisia picked small pieces of hay that clung to it. In the dark she heard Papa's deep breathing and then Stefan's as he fell asleep by her side.

Wide-awake, too excited to sleep, Marisia remembered the train they'd taken that morning. It had clat-tered along the rails at unimaginable speeds, snorting, tossing black smoke into the air.

Without a sound Marisia shoved the quilt aside and crept to the window. In the street below a couple passed arm in arm. What were they doing up so late? In a neighboring building a man shouted. Somewhere in this great city the lady in the carriage must be sleeping.

Marisia moved to the table and lit a candle. In its dim

light she searched through her things until she found the set of pencils Grandma had given her. She spread her paper out on the uneven surface of the table and bent over it.

For an hour Marisia sketched, working to catch on paper the haughty look and all the finery of her lady. Only when Mama stirred restlessly and started to wake did Marisia blow out the candle. She crept across the room and lay down. Beneath her quilt, she could feel the floor's rough planks.

If only she could sink deep into a plump feather bed with silk covers, like her lady's bed, Marisia thought. If only she could ride in a fine carriage pulled by a matched pair of horses.

Katrina's cough disturbed Marisia's fantasy. In real life, Marisia reminded herself, she churned butter, pressed apples for cider, ground poppy seeds, dipped candles, made the beds, swept the floor, stored vegetables in the root cellar or went to fetch them out. She beat rugs, threshed wheat, and stirred the lye to make soap. Along wet paths that muddied her skirts, she drove their two cows to the shed for milking. She'd never had a servant or sipped from a golden goblet or worn a velvet cape.

Moonlight moved across the windowsill and came into the room.

"Anything is possible in America," Papa had said once. Was that true? What had Elsa told her about all the gold in America?

It was one of Elsa's crazy stories, recited after dark by a fire they'd built one night near the stream. She and

Adam and Katrina had listened while the dogs nuzzled up next to them, seeming to listen too, their eyes glowing in the fire's flames.

"Everywhere in America there's gold," Elsa had said. "In Alaska men dig it out of the ice. Hundreds of men freeze each year trying to get at it. All across the miles of ice in that frozen land you can see their corpses with the ice picks sticking straight up in the air. Petrified, that's what those men are, petrified for all time. They're frozen there for all eternity because of their own greed."

Over them bats had flown. The ancient, dappled horse that they had tethered close by shuffled nervously.

"And in the West, in California," Elsa had gone on in the raspy whisper she used for stories like this one, "there are men who haul gold nuggets in great buckets straight out of the mountains. If they don't find gold, the bosses punish them. They whip them or even hang them from trees to die. Late at night, on nights just like this, you can hear their skeletons. They whirl around and around and around in the wind and chime like bells."

"You're making this up," Adam declared. He bit at his thumbnail.

Luckily, Katrina seemed to understand little of Elsa's story. She lifted the flap of the black dog's ear and blew a stream of air straight into it. The dog shook his head. He snorted in disgust. Katrina blew into his ear again.

"I'm not making it up," Elsa swore. "You can ride through that country on a horse and see the skeletons hanging there. People can hear the chiming of the bones for miles around."

In spite of herself, Marisia would feel the need to pull one of the dogs closer to her for comfort, though she'd never have admitted it.

That night Elsa had told them another thing. "This part is really true, I swear, Marisia. It's not just a story. My cousin—you know, Celia—received a letter from a girl in New York City where you're going. The girl saw some streets there that were paved in gold. They have so much gold in America that they pave streets with it. Can you believe that? Nothing will ever happen to me in this village, Marisia, but in America you'll be strolling along streets of gold. Oh, you have to write letters to me and tell me about everything. Promise."

Before they boarded the boat, she would send Elsa a letter, Marisia told herself. From America she would send Elsa dozens more.

On the street below the room, horse hooves sounded. Those hooves clanked as drearily as Elsa's skeletons did. Moments later came someone's boisterous, drunken singing. The song was a German song, and Marisia could understand none of it.

CHAPTER THREE

Marisia watched the gulls, who tried as hard as they could to follow the boat but were held back by a stiff wind. In a long line they bobbed up and down, flapping their wings and complaining angrily.

"Look at them," she said to Stefan. "They remind me of that woman who'd shriek and scold so much at the market when we were selling fruit there. Remember? The one who'd come with her fat little twins." That woman had always pinched at their pears and apples with her stubby fingers and glared at them with small, black, birdlike eyes.

Stefan leaned over the side of the boat. Like a rough hand, the wind tousled his reddish hair. "They'll turn back soon, the gulls will. They can't follow us for long. They need to have a place to land."

In the harbor, the people standing on the piers grew smaller and smaller until they were only spots of color. In an hour the distant land looked like nothing more than a thin wisp of fog, and then the birds disappeared the way Stefan said they would.

In front of the ship's prow a path of bright sun twisted through the tumbling waves. This path would lead them  to a strange land. Her life was changing the way lives changed in the stories Mama had told her when she was small, by the quick wave of a magician's wand that could chase away familiar things and make fantastic ones appear. As if reading Marisia's thoughts, Stefan said, "In the new world I'll never have to hide again. Mama won't have to worry about Papa's saying what he thinks. It'll be different there."

At noon a gong sounded, and the people on the boat lined up with the tin plates and spoons they were given for their meal. "Those cooking pots they're using," Stefan said, "they're so big, you could cook people in them."

Near the head of the line Marisia noticed a girl whose glossy black hair flowed in curling waves down her perfectly straight back. With wide cheeks and clear skin her face was like a storybook face. An old man stared at her, his mouth agape, as if he were trying to decide whether or not she was real. A boy in short pants and a long, dark coat grabbed onto the girl's leg. The girl bent over and swept his hair out of his eyes.

What would it be like to be so perfect? What if everything about you were flawless—your nose and eyes, the way you held your plate, your gliding walk? Marisia ran a finger along the uneven line of her own nose, which was too long, she thought. Elsa said that she had hair like sun on the leaves in the fall and that she could talk with her eyes and say anything she wanted without saying one word. But did any of that matter?

Was Elsa saying she was pretty or not?

Marisia couldn't ever make up her own mind. Sometimes she felt as if she were pretty. Other times she felt awkward and plain, her arms too dark from sun, her mouth too large, her hair unkempt. She caught her narrow waist in both her hands and squeezed it to reassure herself. After all, she liked her waist.

"Marisia, come, the line is moving." Papa nudged her.

When their turns came, a man ladled a stew onto their plates. It was made up more of thin gravy than of anything solid. Another sailor handed out chunks of a dry brown bread. Hungry, Marisia bit into one.

"Wait until we all sit before you begin, Marisia."

"But Mama, I'm hungry."

"You're always hungry, but wait."

"Oh, Mama." Marisia's thick brows bunched together and her wide-set blue eyes heated up. If she said anything to Mama, Papa would tell her to behave herself. She pursed her lips closed. It felt as if someone had stitched her mouth shut. Why was Mama always the one who was right?

Katrina poked Marisia with her elbow and pointed to the deck above them. There circling women held white parasols over their heads. Adam craned his thin neck to peer upwards too. "Who are they, Papa?"

"That's first class." Papa tucked in Adam's shirt, which had slipped out of the waist of his brown knickers. "They're going to America just like us, but they have cabins, and those men dressed in white serve them."

"Can we go up there?" When Mama shook her head no, Katrina pursed her mouth in displeasure.

"It's for fancy people," Stefan told Katrina, "not for us. They sleep in real beds up there. They have wine with dinner and candles on tables that are covered by white tablecloths."

"The important thing is that we're all going to America," Mama said. "If we go steerage or first class or second class, what does it matter?"

Marisia wanted to say that she would give almost anything in the world to have candles and servants. Instead she took the apple Mama passed her. Slipping it into her pocket, she rose. Down the ship's deck she strolled. All around her were strangers. One of them was a beefy man who coaxed notes from a fiddle with his bow while, stomach jiggling, he hopped up and down to his own tune.

Passing him, Marisia rounded the deck. She stepped out onto the ship's stern, where a sharp gust of air hit her with such force that she stopped for a moment. The sudden, biting cold made her eyes water. She blinked away the tears and saw that this wind-swept space was deserted except for one other person—a small boy in a dark coat, the boy who'd been with the black-haired girl. He was doing what he shouldn't be doing. He had climbed onto a high platform that rose above the ship's railing. On that platform a lifeboat was fastened to stout poles. As Marisia watched, the boy began to shimmy up a pole. In his black coat, creeping upward, he looked like a little spider.

Marisia cried out to him. "You can't go up there!" She ran until she was at the rail below him. "You can't go up there, I said!"

Now the boy tossed one leg into the boat and hoisted himself up. The wind blew his hair up into sand-colored tufts. Straddling the side of the boat, he peered down at her.

"Come down. I'm telling you it's not safe."

As Marisia spoke, two things happened. The boy shook his head in refusal and a giant wave slapped at the ship. When the ship pitched, the boy tumbled sideways and disappeared from view. Marisia stared at the empty space where he'd been. She held her breath. Then there the boy was again, plopped down on the seat in the lifeboat's prow. She let her breath out. She took another and called, "Hold on!"

He didn't. Instead, bouncing up and down on the seat, he flapped his arms like a bird in flight. Fifteen feet below the boy's perch, the ocean coiled into black waves. "Hold on," Marisia called again. Still he ignored her.

She held up the apple that Mama had given her. "I'll

give you an apple if you let me come up too. It's a special apple from our own orchard."

The boy stared at it, a grin on his face.

On the wet railing Marisia's feet slipped. She clutched a line of rope and pulled herself up. The ship mounted a cresting wave, tilted, and simply spilled her onto the platform as if she were a bag of oats that was being delivered. She squirmed forward. She managed to stand and grasp onto the sides of the lifeboat, but then another enormous wave hit them, and she could go no further. She saw the boy's upturned face and open mouth, as he was thrown across the seat to the ocean side. Marisia lunged for him. Her fingers clenched at his coat. With all her might she jerked at it. She tugged the boy toward her. She caught his elbow.

Keeping her grasp on the boy, Marisia hoisted her body over the side of the boat and slipped onto the seat beside him. Underneath them, like fists, waves pummeled the ship. Cold spray drenched her. She wrapped her arms around the boy's chunky body.

"You said you'd give me the apple," he shouted.

"I will, but we have to go down. It's dangerous up here. You could have fallen into that water. Look at it, " she said. "Do you know how cold and deep that water is?" She put the apple in the boy's hand. She ran a hand over the skirt of her dress. Soaked with spray, it lay across her legs like a heavy blanket.

The boy took a bite of the apple. His head turned. He jumped. "Father!" he shouted out in a piping voice. "Father! It's me! Up here! See me?"

On the deck, a bearded man ran toward them, an astonished look on his face. "What are you doing? I've been looking everywhere for you. What in the name of heaven are you doing up there?"

"We're playing! See? She gave me an apple!"

"By all that is holy! Bring him down. Bring him down immediately."

"I was trying to help him," Marisia began to explain. "When I walked by, he—"

The man's words fired at her like shots from a rifle. "Immediately, I said. Do as you're told. Now!"

As ordered, gripping the boy, Marisia climbed over the side of the lifeboat. At the edge of the platform she lowered him into the man's arms, which were as stout as a bear's. His face was a bear's too, with its massive beard and mustache and brows, with barely any human flesh visible. He even shook the boy like a bear would have done, until the boy's head whipped back and forth on the end of his neck. Like broken wings, the boy's arms flopped at his sides.

"You shouldn't run off. Do you hear me? And you!" The man's cloudy face turned toward Marisia. His mouth puffed out. "Where is your sense? Of all the stupidities!"

"But it isn't what—"

"You come near my son again, I'll see that you're horsewhipped. Do you hear me?" The man whirled away, dragging the boy by the collar of his coat the way someone would drag a dog. Tripping, choking, the boy cried out.

She wouldn't be able to explain anything to this squat

man Marisia knew. Nor could the boy tell the true story. What had he really understood of it? She pulled at a large splinter tucked into her thumb. When it came out, blood trickled after it.

Well, she told herself, she wouldn't stay here, chilled to the bone in her wet clothes, worrying about this like a fool. She stepped onto the railing and leapt forward. With a hard thud that hurt her ankle, she landed on the deck. Marisia straightened. She turned her back on a bullying wind that shoved her forward and thought of the man's gruff voice and of his threat to whip her.

In the ship's hold Marisia gathered dry clothes out from under her bunk and took off her wet dress. The skin along her arms was covered with goose bumps. She changed, hung up her damp things, and sat on her bunk. In front of her was a rumpled wall made of old blankets that hung from a rope. The wall of blankets ran down the middle of these murky quarters and separated the women's area from the men's. On the other side of it, a man shouted at someone else. On her own side, in the next aisle, two girls bent their heads together, talking in Yiddish, their voices excited.

One girl had a dark braid that swung back and forth when she shook her head. Suddenly she broke into laughter. Holding her stomach, unable to breathe for laughing, she fell back on the bed and rolled from side to side.

At the sight, Marisia was pierced with loneliness for Elsa. If Elsa were here, she would understand everything. She would be furious at the bearded man. "He's an ogre, a tyrant!" Elsa would declare, siding at once with Marisia because they were best friends.

If Elsa were here, they would talk until Marisia's hurt feelings flew away, the way birds did when Mama chased them from the seeded furrows in the garden.

But Elsa was not here. There was no one to take her part.

Marisia drew her bundle of things from underneath her bunk. From the bundle she took her picture of the lady in the carriage and spread it on the bed. If she had no one else, she had her lady.

With a gold pencil Marisia brushed at her lady's pearls until they seemed to catch the light's reflection. With a black pencil she shaded in a shadow at her lady's neck.

"I wish I could draw."

The soft voice startled Marisia, who looked up to see the black-haired girl. The girl evaded Marisia's gaze, staring down at her own high-topped, buttoned shoes. She said, "I shouldn't be here. Papa pointed you out up on the deck. He told us we couldn't talk to you." The girl wiped her hands on the side of her skirt as if, in speaking to Marisia, she'd dirtied them. Then she moved past Marisia along the narrow aisle.

Indifferently, as if none of this mattered to her, Marisia spoke to the girl's retreating figure. "Your brother was about to fall out of that lifeboat. I wanted to bring him down."

The girl turned. "Bring Casimir down?"

Marisia picked up a colored pencil, ignoring her.

A minute passed. The dove-gray dress grazed the side of Marisia's bunk. "Please speak to me."

If she brushed silver into the eyes of the lady, would it bring back the proud look she'd worn? She would be as proud as this herself, Marisia determined, so proud that nobody could hurt her ever again—certainly not this girl. Marisia heard the shuffling of the girl's shoes on the wooden planks. She made a dozen quick strokes with her pencil.

"How can you know just what to do to make your drawing come alive like that?"

Without looking up, Marisia said, "I told your brother to come down. He wouldn't. Of course I climbed up there to get him. I have a little sister who's always doing stupid things like that, too. Your brother could have fallen overboard."

"You didn't bring Casimir up there to play with him?"

"What did I just tell you?" Indignant, Marisia looked up. "How could anyone think that?"

The girl's face flushed. "I don't know. It's only what Father told us. Father said...well, Father must have thought..."

"Your father doesn't stop to listen to anyone. I tried to explain!"

"If a mistake has been made..." Without finishing the sentence the girl clasped her hands together in front of her. Her fingernails were as clear as glass. Marisia looked down at her own square hands with their roughened knuckles. She was tempted to hide them away in the folds of her skirt so the girl wouldn't see them.

"Don't stop drawing. I like to watch," the girl told her.

Marisia scratched away a piece of dirt at the corner of her paper and leaned close to trace thin lines of lace at the neckline of her lady's dress.

"They gave me art lessons once to make me into a lady, but I was never much good at it," the girl said.

"Your parents?"

"Yes." She smoothed back her black hair, which had fallen forward. It was like a piece of silk. She had a high forehead, like Mama's.

"Why did they want you to be a lady?"

"It's hard to explain really, but when I was a little girl, I was so beautiful that people would stop and stare at me in the streets my father says. That put ideas into his head. He thought I'd make a very good marriage if he gave me the chance, so he did—give me the chance I mean—with all kinds of lessons, French and art and music and embroidery lessons." The girl's voice had a slight stutter, as if long ago she'd been trained out of one. It sounded hollow, too, Marisia thought, like an echo of someone else's voice.

"In America," the girl went on, "Father says I can marry far better than I ever could in Poland. He says girls who have no money at all marry into the upper classes there. If that happens, Father thinks we'll do very well. He says it will happen. I'm sixteen now, old enough for marriage, and he says the Americans have never seen anything like me." She shrugged, as if to say that she'd had no choice in the matter. She was putting her beauty aside, Marisia realized, the way someone would put aside a book or a spoon—as if it weren't important at all.

Marisia put her pencils down, more interested in this story than in her lady. "Is that why your family decided to leave? To marry you off?"

"No," the girl shook her head. "The truth is that last year Father ran up terrible debts. It wasn't his fault. He made investments, you see, but people cheated him. Afterwards he had to sell his shop to pay what he owed or go to prison—it was a butcher shop. He decided that if he had to start over again, he'd start over in America."

"In New York?" Marisia asked.

The girl nodded. "We'll live with my uncle. He left Poland thirteen years ago. He's been successful. He wants Father to be the butcher in his grocery store."

She stopped talking and looked down. When she looked at Marisia again, her skin was flushed. "My name is Sofia, Sofia Cybulski," she stammered. "I can tell Mother the truth about Casimir and the lifeboat. She could speak to Father, I suppose, but even if she did, I don't think he'd let me speak to you."

"Why not? Once he knew what happened, why wouldn't...."

"Don't be mad. It's Father's way. He doesn't like to change his mind. No one can change him, Mother says."

Marisia felt her face flush hot with anger. "It's not right!"

Sofia's face was very still, the only movement the irregular shuddering of her eyelids. She set her thumb-nail under another nail, snapping it up to make tiny clicking sounds—they were the sounds an insect might make. "My mother married when she was fifteen, a year younger than I am. She says she never questioned her own father and she's never questioned my father. I should do the same, not question what I'm told."

"Mama and Papa, they don't teach me that," Marisia blurted out. "About obeying everybody, I mean. Maybe it's because of my grandfather, of what happened to him when Mama was little."

She slowed her hurrying voice down. "I'll tell you the story if you want me to," and Marisia went on when Sofia nodded.

"When Mama was very young, when she was seven or eight, there was a drought where we live. Crops failed. People didn't have enough to eat, so the farmers wouldn't give up their crops to the Russian soldiers who came. They fought instead. My grandfather, too. The rebellion was put down. All of the peasants had to give up their weapons—not even weapons really, only the scythes they used to mow hay, or their rakes and shovels. So you see, they were defenseless.

"That didn't matter. By the czar's orders they were all killed. The soldiers shot all of them, and after they were done, the soldiers heaped the bodies in a huge trench. They couldn't even find Grandfather's body afterwards Mama says. Grandma was never able to give him a proper burial." Marisia stopped. She remembered how Mama's voice would shake whenever she told this same story about Grandfather and how Grandma would never speak of it. "Mama's never obeyed the czar and learned Russian. She won't. She won't do it."

Sofia stared at her for a long time without speaking,

her back perfectly straight, as if held in place by a rod. Then she shuffled her hands in her lap and leaned forward. "I'll be your friend, no matter what. I'll be your friend even if it displeases Father." The edges of her mouth twitched.

What a serious, earnest, strange creature she was! Marisia pulled Sofia from the edge of the bed, where she'd perched to hear the story, into its center, right next to her own crossed legs. Their knees touched. "We can keep our friendship secret if your father's going to get mad at you for being friends with me."

"If he ever finds out ..." Sofia started to speak, then stopped. Her arms outstretched to brace herself on the bed, she studied the makeshift curtain that separated them from the men's section of the hold. She seemed to be looking right through the blankets that hung along that line of rope. Was Sofia seeing her father, that bearlike man with the glowering eyes?

"Sofia, what is it?"

Sofia didn't answer. Still staring, she was silent and rigid. Her skin was as white as porcelain. A chill raced along Marisia's spine. What sort of man cast a spell on his own daughter like this, so that all signs of life left her?

"Sofia!" At the call, Sofia woke from her trance.

"What happened?" Marisia asked. "Is it your father?"

"I must go. Mother will be wondering where I am." Sofia's mouth quivered. She stood and ran her hands over her rumpled skirt to straighten it. "I must go," she said again in her muffled voice. She hurried down the aisle as if she were fleeing for her life. Marisia stared after her.

Chapter Four

O<small>N THE THIRD MORNING AT SEA</small>, the air grew heavy. Like ragged clothes on a line, clouds hung at the edge of the sky. Waves grew taller. By noon they were as high as the ceiling of a room. The day darkened. Marisia listened to thunder that grumbled at her from the horizon, where lightning flashed in quavering lines.

On the deck a sailor swayed back and forth as he walked, his arms stretched out. He looked like a picture Marisia had once seen of a circus man on a tightrope. As he approached, he shouted something at her, but the wind scattered his words. Only when he put his mouth near Marisia's ear could she hear him. "Get below. Move along now."

Three or four times Marisia slipped on the wet deck, and once the sailor grabbed her elbow to keep her from falling. Clouds swirled overhead, now as thick as porridge in a pot. Just as she reached the door to the hold, rain broke and descended in a solid curtain from the sky.

She turned to look, but the sailor forced the door open and pushed her through. "It's a bad one, a gale. You stay below," he said crossly, his clammy hand on her shoulder.

Abruptly she answered, "Don't shove me."

"Miss, you listen to me now. People go down in seas like this, straight down to the bottom like rocks. It'll be you if you don't do what I say and get below." The locks of hair sticking out all along the edges of his blue knit cap lashed about angrily. He slammed the door in her face. Who was he to order her around like that? Marisia thought. She opened the door once more and peeked

 outside. Just then a wave slammed over the deck and came straight at her. Quickly she shut the door against it.

All that day the ship tossed in the storm. Across from Marisia's bunk Mama huddled with Katrina and sang senseless nursery rhymes to her. Mama's egg-shaped face was as pale as an egg. Even her lips were bleached of color. "What's wrong? Are you sick, Mama?" Marisia asked her.

"I wish this rocking would stop. I feel as if we've been swallowed by a whale. Like Jonah in the Bible when the whale swallowed him whole." She held her stomach with both hands. There were blue circles under her eyes.

"Well, lucky for us, God saved Jonah from the stomach of the whale. Remember that," Marisia said. But Mama was right, Marisia knew. They'd been gulped right up. Inside this monster's stomach the light was so faint Marisia could hardly see, the air so close and tight, she could hardly breathe.

"Lie down, Mama. I'll take care of Katrina." When Mama lay back, Marisia pulled the quilt over her.

"The engines. The thudding. It's like drums that never stop." Wearily Mama covered her eyes with her hand. "My head," she murmured.

Marisia took Katrina from Mama. Katrina squirmed out of Marisia's arms and fell, her knee hitting a corner of the bunk. She yelped and then began to cry in sobs that mixed with coughing.

"Stay here, Katrina, on my bed," Marisia said, lifting her up.

Now Sofia came down into the hold and sat with them. She bent her head and took a deep breath.

"Are you all right?" asked Marisia.

"It's this rolling. Someone told me that even the sailors are getting seasick."

"Stefan says Adam can't stop throwing up, Mama's sick, and I feel queasy too. I hate this storm." Marisia grabbed Sofia's hand. "It's so stuffy in here, it stinks. I can't stand it. Come on. At least we can open the door for a minute and breathe real air."

"Me too," Katrina shouted out.

"You can't, Katrina. Stay here. Don't whine at me like that," Marisia added irritably. "I told you two stories, didn't I? We've made all these little paper dolls. You're acting like a baby."

"Don't," Sofia said. "She's only little."

"She's a pest sometimes. Doesn't Casimir ever pester you? You're too good—that's your problem."

Sofia stared at Marisia until Marisia said, "I didn't mean that."

"No, you did mean it. Maybe you're right. Nobody ever lets me be bad, not ever, so maybe I'm too good."

Their arms around each other's waists to keep from falling, Sofia and Marisia went to the top of the stairs. Marisia slipped the door open an inch. Wet air whistled through the crack. They breathed the air in.

Marisia opened the door another inch. Outside, the rain came down in whipping sheets. Waves jumped the ship's railing and splintered into pieces on the deck. Like a cradle rocked by a hand gone completely mad, the ship pitched from side to side. Marisia clung to the wall. Her stomach heaved, and she closed her eyes. Her face was cold, but Marisia felt herself perspiring. She wiped sweat from her forehead.

What had the sailor said? "People go down in seas like this. They go straight down to the bottom like rocks."

Would they all die out here in this ocean and sink one by one to the ocean floor, where crabs could claw at their eyes and swirling sharks devour them? Gagging, Marisia opened her eyes again and threw the door open as wide as she could. She leaned forward to vomit. The vomit blew back in the wind. Specks of it sprinkled across her dress. She gasped for air and took another step forward, vomiting a second time. Just then a wave lifted the ship as if it were no heavier than a leaf floating in a pond and hurled it to one side. Marisia stumbled. Her foot caught. She fell to the deck, smashing her head. There was a ringing in her ears, the taste of blood in her mouth, the pelting of the heavy rain.

Marisia twisted and looked back. Screaming Marisia's name, Sofia stepped out of the hold. Marisia struggled to her hands and knees, but when she tried to crawl up the deck's tilting surface toward Sofia and safety, she slipped on the wet planks. Helpless, she could only crouch in place and stare at her friend.

She saw how Sofia took another step away from the hold. In the wind her skirt ballooned and seemed to lift her up. With her arms extended, she looked strangely graceful, like a skater on ice. That odd thought careened through Marisia's dizzy brain just as Sofia tottered, like a skater would. Then, falling straight forward, Sofia went down.

On her belly, Sofia slid along the steep, slick deck. With her arms thrust out before her, she tried to stop herself. She couldn't. She came closer and closer. Marisia could see her face. Sofia's eyes were shut tight, but her mouth was wide open. She seemed to be screaming, but there was no sound. When Marisia grabbed at her sleeve, Sofia's eyes opened. They were filled with terror. The sleeve tore from Marisia's grasp. Sofia slid past her.

Marisia told herself to wake from this nightmare. She knew she must. Crouching low, she crawled after Sofia.

The ship's railing stopped Sofia's careening slide, but one of her legs went under the railing. Like an animal poked by knives, Sofia thrashed. Over the wind and the awful creaking of the ship came her squeal.

Marisia slithered forward, arm still stretched out to Sofia, who was not in reach, whose other leg—Marisia saw it now—was slipping under the railing too. "Sofia! No! Sofia!"

A wave rose, side-swiping the ship, lifting it. Sofia still lay half on the deck and half off, her legs underneath the railing as before. Then as the wave rose higher, the ship leaned for an instant away from the sea. The deck, which had tilted down, now tilted up. Sofia pushed herself back from the railing.

Marisia brushed wet hair out of her eyes. "Hurry!" she cried. "Hurry, Sofia!"

In a sitting position, propelling herself with hands and feet, Sofia scooted toward Marisia. Marisia could see the line of teeth in her mouth. She could hear Sofia call, "Inside! Now!"

Again and again the steerage door smashed against the ship's side. It made the noise a great, tolling bell would make. Side by side, she and Sofia were crawling toward it.

For more than a minute they stood where they were. Marisia could hear her own hard breathing and Sofia's. She felt as if a hand held her by the throat and refused to release her.

"You know how close we were to death? This close," Sofia finally said, fingers almost touching. "This close." Below the gold locket that hung around her neck, a thin vein pulsed. Strands of dripping hair curled like snakes around her face.

"You went out there on that deck to help me. You didn't have to," Marisia said. She wiped at the dirt on Sofia's face with the sleeve of her own dress. Sofia's lip was swollen, the neck of her dress torn; even her blue eyes seemed darker, as if muddied.

Sofia pushed Marisia's arm away. "I'm dirty. For once in my life I'm dirty. Let it be." Marisia saw her unfasten the locket that hung by a gold chain around her neck. "Keep this," she said. "I want you to have it." She slipped it into Marisia's hand.

Marisia thought to ask why she should have a gift but the words didn't come.

From the doorway they could smell the awful stench of the hold. Others had been sick. They heard groaning and cries. Marisia took one step down into the darkness, then stopped, dizzy. She sat with a thump.

Sofia sat beside her. She closed her hand around Marisia's. The ship shook. "I don't want to go down either," she whispered. "It's like walking into a trap."

That night Marisia woke often. Her arm hurt terribly, and she wondered if she had cracked a bone. Continually from a bunk nearby, a broken voice murmured, "God save us, God save us."

The ship's engines thudded and strained, but it seemed to Marisia that the ship went up and down and never forward, as if it were chained in place.

In her dream the ship darted back and forth like a

scared rabbit until, in the end, waves devoured it. She found in the morning that, in a way, the dream had been true. A rumor ran through the hold—that three sailors had been swept overboard during the night and were lost to the sea.

By mid-morning there was a change in the weather. The winds decreased. The terrible throbbing of the seas died back. Crew arrived and left loaves of hard rye bread and a great barrel of pickled herring in the hold. Those who could—those who were not too sick—ate.

Marisia brought Mama a cup of water and a hunk of bread, but Mama wouldn't touch either one. All color erased from her face, she lay weakly on the bunk.

In the tiny washroom Marisia ran cold salt water from the spigot in the sink to wash out a rag. By now the little room smelled unbearable and the sink was filthy. Returning to Mama, Marisia washed her face with the rag as best she could and asked, "Will you be all right, Mama?"

Mama nodded and patted Marisia's knee. "People don't die of seasickness. I'll be fine. Go." Marisia stared at Mama, frightened, then left.

"Mama hasn't eaten at all," Marisia told Sofia. "She looks half-dead. I wish there was something to give her besides bread and herring. I never want to eat herring again."

Katrina crawled into Marisia's lap. With her two pointer fingers she pulled her lips wide to make a face. She growled.

"Father says they have cherries in first class," Sofia said. "They serve bowls of them."

A chain kept passengers from the inside stairs that led to the higher decks. "That sign says No Admittance," Sofia announced.

"But I can't read German like you can."

"You'll ignore me if I tell you again not to do this, won't you?"

"Don't be so serious," Marisia laughed. She ran her hands over the dress they had taken from the large trunk that held Sofia's best things. "I've never worn anything like this."

"It fits you perfectly, except for the length."

"This taffeta feels like flower petals."

"Hurry! Someone's coming!" Sofia pushed Marisia under the chain.

Marisia ran up the stairs. She pushed through a swinging door, found more stairs, and climbed those. They led to a long corridor. At the end of the corridor a gentleman stepped from a cabin and turned in her direction. He seemed to glare at her. Did he know she didn't belong here? The pins Sofia had stuck into the skirt to shorten it pricked at her ankles.

The gentleman came so close Marisia could smell the cigar smoke that clung to his clothes. Just then he tipped his hat and smiled, revealing a large row of protruding teeth. "Good day, miss."

On she went, tossed from side to side by the rocking boat. At last a passageway opened into a large room where, on a table, Marisia saw rows of teacups, bowls of sugar, slices of lemon, trays of cakes, sliced bread, cheeses, and fruit, including the cherries she wanted for Mama. As Marisia pointed first at one thing and then at another, a waiter put them on the plate she held.

When the plate was full, she retreated to a corner. Only two other people were in the room, a very fat Russian women and a young man. They paid no attention to Marisia. They didn't see her slip most of the food from the plate into the pockets she and Sofia had sewn into the dress, slitting the side seams in its full skirt to create an opening.

In half an hour she returned to the table. She returned a third time. Inspecting Marisia, the waiter smoothed his straight black mustache with the tip of one finger. She said, "I've been so sick from the storm that I haven't eaten, not for days. I'm weak from hunger." The waiter rolled his eyes sympathetically and insisted she drink tea.

"Halfway only, halfway or spilling," he said in uncertain Russian, handing her a cup. "Please," he said and offered cream and sugar. Marisia sipped at the pale, sweet, steaming mixture.

"Where did you find this food?" Mama asked.

"Sofia's father got it from a sailor." Marisia crossed her fingers behind her back against the lie she told. "Sofia wants to share with us."

"Cherries!" Mama said, holding one. "Oh, fresh food is wonderful, but no more. My stomach is still so unsettled. Marisia, bring some of these cherries to Stefan and Adam and your father."

Sofia fed Katrina bits of a soft cheese that they'd never

before tasted. Katrina tipped her head back and opened her mouth. "You're a baby bird," Sofia told her.

The next day Marisia climbed the stairs a second time. She filled her pockets with bread, cheese, slices of chicken, and a sausage turnover. When she gave the food to Mama, Mama smiled at her and ate.

When Marisia went up the stairs a third time, the weather had shifted. After days of crashing against the boat, the waves now swelled listlessly. In the dining room dozens of people circled about. A beautiful boy of six sat on the edge of the brown velvet couch. Bright ringlets of hair reached to his shoulders. A woman dressed in black, taller than most of the men, kept her hand on a diamond brooch pinned at her neck as if afraid someone might snatch it. A girl her own age passed by, a straw hat perched on her head.

Backing against a wall, Marisia looked carefully about her and quickly slipped away six cherries, a slice of buttered bread, and a tart. When she turned from the wall, she saw the old woman with the diamond brooch looking directly at her. She had a long, stiff nose and a head that bobbed angrily.

Caught in the woman's glare, Marisia felt her face grow hot. The woman walked toward the ship's steward. She talked to him and pointed at Marisia. The steward nodded.

Marisia stepped behind two men. The steward had started to move in her direction. Before he could reach her, she was through the door. Moving rapidly, she squeezed past a mother with four children. Behind her

Marisia heard their soft chattering fade and then the steward's rapid footsteps. A voice fired German words. She knew the words were aimed at her, but she ignored them and went on.

Coming to a corridor, she turned left. Bending, she slipped off her shoes and in stockinged feet that made no sound, Marisia ran. At the end of the corridor, she turned right. Where did this passageway lead? Not far behind footsteps pounded. She heard a shout and an answering call. She turned left into another passageway. Finally, ahead of her, she saw double doors that led outside. She darted forward and bolted through them.

In drizzling rain, gripping the railing, tipping forward, Marisia raced down metal stairs. A door opened above her and feet hammered. Making herself as small as she could, Marisia pulled her gown into a tight ball around her knees and squeezed under the staircase. Feet crashed directly over her head. She saw the back of the steward's white uniform and his black boots.

Twice the man stomped back and forth. Then he disappeared. Marisia moved a numb leg. There was no human sound, only waves, wind, and the constant tapping of rain. She backed out of her hiding place. There was no one in sight. Holding her shoes and pulling up her wet dress, she dashed for the steps that would take her down to the steerage hold.

Without warning, a sailor stepped directly in front of her. When Marisia tried to duck away from him, his hand circled her wrist like a noose. He spat out German words she couldn't understand.

"I don't speak German," she said in Polish.

"You're the girl they're looking for. They said you must belong in steerage class." He spoke in Polish. For the first time she looked at this stranger. He was not so very tall, but he was large with a barrel-chest and thick neck. The skin of his face was rough and pockmarked; the whites of his eyes were flecked with tiny red spots, like bits of blood.

"I'm the girl they're looking for...yes, it's me." Marisia tried to keep her voice steady, but it broke. She shook the water from her grimy skirts.

"What did you take?"

"Food."

"What? Speak so I can hear you!"

"Food," she repeated over the lump in her own throat.

"Food? And what else? They said you'd been stealing."

From her pocket Marisia took wet pieces of buttered bread, the cherries, and the broken tart. She held them out.

"Why? They feed you down below, don't they? Not good enough for you?"

In answer Marisia only bit her lip. Then the words tumbled from her mouth. "It was the herring. It's all we've had since the storm began."

The sailor stared harshly at Marisia before he spoke. "Herring. There's worse than herring in store for you if they catch you stealing. They'll land the ship, but they won't let you get off it. You'll make the voyage all over again next week—this time in the other direction. They won't send back a girl by herself, either. They'll return the whole family. Now how do you feel about that? All because you don't like herring!"

"But they can't!"

"And what makes you think they can't?" the sailor asked in a cold voice, folding his thick arms over his chest. "They can do whatever they like with you."

Goose bumps covered Marisia's arms. She rubbed them hard, but still she shivered. "If my brother goes back to Poland," she said, "they'll shoot him."

The sailor pulled at his cap and glared so intently Marisia thought he was going to strike her. After a long pause he spoke. "I won't ask why. I can guess at their reasons. I escaped Poland twenty-three years ago when I was younger than you are. The czar decided to wipe out the Jews in my village, Jews like me." The sailor's mouth flattened into a thin line. When he spoke again, his voice was cold. "Half of our people were killed. Houses burned down. People shot. Worse than that. I saw soldiers do such terrible things, I try not to remember any of it."

He jerked his head twice from side to side. "I won't keep you out of America because of some cherries and bread," he whispered in a gritty voice. "I'm not going to have anybody shot on my account." He stepped past Marisia as if she weren't there. He took two long strides.

"I'll remember you. God take care of you," Marisia stammered after him.

He turned back. The eyes were still hard. "God? First I'll count on you to take care of me. I'm telling you that. I count on God only when there's nobody else to count on. If someone else catches you, don't mention my part in this."

"No," she said, "I promise you that I'll never..."

But he was gone before she could complete her promise.

She thought back to the driver of the cart, who had got them past the border guard with his awful pitchfork. Now there was this sailor. Twice now, when falling, she'd been saved by a net spread by others to catch her.

The next day the ocean's surface flattened and the sun was bright. On the deck, to wild accordion music, a man waltzed a little girl who barely came up to his waist. People clapped time for them. Beyond the dancers Katrina and Adam played leapfrog with a ragged, thin boy who shouted without stopping in a language Marisia couldn't even identify.

Stefan was at her side, his arms crossed. Light glinted on his reddened hair so it shone like copper. It flashed across his face, across the uneven nose that was like her own and the long mouth that was also like hers. The brim of his cap cast a shadow that hid his eyes. A pretty girl passed, staring at Stefan with an interest that made Marisia want to laugh, but Stefan didn't seem even to notice her. Suddenly he scowled. "The sailors say we almost didn't make it," he said. "That first night of the storm, you know what? One of the sailors told me it was a hurricane and that they were worried about the boat's sinking. One of the worst storms they've seen. And those three sailors who went overboard that night? One was sixteen, that's all."

Stefan fell silent. Marisia looked behind the ship at the

dark, tipping water that now held the three sailors—they would never hear this music or feel the heat of this sun.

At midday gulls flew behind the boat. In the distance foghorns sounded. Excitedly people gathered their children and searched for their papers and built mountainous piles of belongings on the deck. A fat woman sat on top of one, a toothless smile on her face, a shawl fastened under her chin.

At the railing, with the wind tangling her hair, Marisia peered ahead. Sun spilled across the endless water, which ruffled up in the wind. Then, taking form bit by bit, as if it were being created by God right before Marisia's eyes, land appeared. Murmuring, calling out, praying, others took up places near her to watch this miracle of creation.

The ship lumbered on through a narrow passage into water that was as smooth as a bolt of rolled-out cloth. As they entered the great harbor, Papa swung Katrina onto his shoulders. He braced himself, his legs spread wide. "There she is now," he called out and pointed to the left. "It's the Statue of Liberty."

Adam pressed forward on his tiptoes to see. Everyone on deck was staring in the same direction as Papa at the statue of a woman who stood tall over all of them like some goddess in a story, her torch in her hand, her mouth firm. Her face was powerful and certain, as if she were reassuring all who passed that they were safe now and that she'd stand guard. People cried out to her as if she were real and could hear them. Mama grabbed Marisia's hand and squeezed it tightly. On her cheeks were excited splotches of color.

The ship lumbered past the Statue of Liberty and headed toward a wedge of land where a fortresslike building rose up. "Ellis Island," someone announced in a baritone voice behind her, but the words meant nothing to Marisia. The sun reddened the building's walls and flickered across its domed turrets.

Beyond that island, in the distance, Marisia could see the dim outline of tall buildings. They looked like giant stakes stuck straight into the ground. Marisia had heard of these skyscrapers but didn't believe that they could really be so high.

Was everything else she'd heard true, too?

Would she be paid in gold coins and earn in a month more money than her family had ever, ever had in their lives? Would she see wild Indians with tomahawks and find Elsa's golden streets? She'd sleep in a feather bed all by herself like Americans did, without Katrina kicking her, the way little girls kicked their big sisters all night long in Poland.

"The czar can't reach us now, no matter how long his arm is," Papa boasted, squinting in the wind, and Mama announced, "We'll be safe today in America." Marisia leaned against Mama, glad she sounded so certain, glad that Papa did. Right now, more than anything else, she wanted for Mama and Papa to know everything there was to know and to be exactly right.

CHAPTER FIVE

Mama's bright red kerchief was tied tightly around her chin. Her face was flushed with excitement. "There you are, Marisia," she said in fretful tones. "I was looking for you. Don't get separated from us!"

"Everybody's getting off, Mama. When will we leave?"

"Not yet. First we go to Ellis Island. In a while they'll send a barge or a ferry to take us there, someone told me. We'll wait for it on that pier."

"But the others are getting off now! Why do we have to wait, Mama?" Marisia demanded.

Before Mama could answer, a heavyset man in front of Marisia turned around and answered for her. "Ellis Island," he said, "that's for the inspection. Those people leaving the ship right now, they're first class passengers. The American government knows they've got money, but you and me and all of these people you see standing here, maybe these ones don't. Maybe they're flat broke. Not a penny, some of 'em, I betcha. What I heard is you need twenty-five dollars or you're not gonna get in."

He held a black bowler hat in his hand and turned it around and around in a circle, faster and faster. "You got to show them twenty-five dollars before they let you into America. They don't want beggars. You got to prove you're not some beggar.

"And you better be fit. Better be ready to work a good, long day. If you can't do that, you shouldn'ta come here in the first place." Like a wind-up toy that had just run down, the man stopped abruptly, snapped his black suspenders, and turned away.

"Do we have enough money to get into America, Mama?" Marisia asked.

"We have enough. It's all right."

"This island, Mama, this Ellis Island, when will we go there?"

Thousands of voices echoed in a dozen languages through the vast hall at Ellis Island, creating a great din, and it seemed to Marisia that the high, curving ceiling was a sky and that under it all the people in the whole wide world were gathered. Some were old. Some were young. Some held children. Some stood alone. Some were determined. Some looked lost and dazed. They glared, laughed, coughed, drank, prayed, cried, shouted, whispered, sneezed, sang, or sat as motionless as statues. Marisia watched three women in embroidered head-dresses who paced back and forth in front of her. Nearby a man slept on a bundle of clothes tied around with a rope, snoring, his hand nestled under his chin, his big chest rising and falling rhythmically.

Checking tags, guards motioned people through iron railings that snaked around and around the room. Marisia  touched the tag pinned to her own coat. On it were their ship's name and her name and a row of numbers she didn't understand. A man shouted at Papa and pointed to a swinging gate. Obediently Papa went through it. Following him, Katrina coughed. Mama leaned over and smoothed her flushed forehead. A few steps further on, when Mama turned aside, a woman standing to the side of the line leaned over Katrina. The woman's hand slashed out and back.

"Papa! A lady put a mark on Katrina's back," Adam called.

Quickly Papa swung Katrina around and said, "I don't know what it means." As he usually did when confused, Papa pulled on his mustache.

At the next gate, without saying a word, a short man in a black coat gripped Marisia's chin. He tilted her head back and forth. He lifted her lips and stared at her teeth and tongue, turned her hands over and pressed her fingernails down until the blood left them, and before Marisia knew what was happening, he snapped her eyelid back with a hook he had in his hand. The jolt of pain brought tears to her eyes. She bit her lip to keep back a cry. He released her. She stared at him and he stared at her, but without really seeing her.

He put a broad hand on Adam's shoulder. "No," Adam said, retreating, nestling against Papa's legs.

"You must," Papa whispered, pushing him toward the man.

Once through that gate, they gathered together. "Why did he do it, Papa?" Adam muttered, rubbing at his eye.

Papa ruffled Adam's hair, then picked Katrina up. "Stay with me," he told them.

They were made to stand in other lines and to sit on benches and to wait in enclosures while the noise of the place rolled over them in great waves. Finally they were led to a woman who took Papa aside. When Papa turned back, he said, "This woman says Katrina must be examined more closely. It's her cough. That's what that blue chalk mark was about. Mama and I will take her. You wait here, all of you. Don't go anywhere."

Marisia huddled on a corner of the bench, keeping an eye on Adam, who knelt and rolled an American penny along the floor. Stefan, half-asleep, leaned back on the bench, his feet sticking out in front of him. From her pocket Marisia drew out the slip of paper on which Sofia had written the address where she would live in New York. She read the words for the hundredth time.

After more than an hour Adam jumped up from the

bench, where he'd finally curled up like a cat. "Look. They're coming!" he yelled.

Papa stood in front of them, his mouth cinched tight. Mama straightened Katrina's dress.

"What is it?" Stefan asked. "What's wrong?"

"They won't let us go any further," Papa said.

Stefan put his hand on Papa's arm. "What do you mean?"

"I can't believe it." Mama untied her scarf from her head and held it in her hands, twisting it and twisting it. "They say it's tuberculosis. What are they talking about? These people here, they don't know anything. It can't be tuberculosis. I won't believe this—in the lungs, like Mrs. Ciorka's husband had, when he kept coughing blood. I won't believe it. The ideas they have in this place, they're crazy."

Mama put a hand on Katrina's head. "I told them if only I could boil herbs for tea and feed her chicken the way I roast it with carrots and noodles, she would get better. It's only all those days on the boat in the storm, the wet air, the cold nights."

"Tuberculosis? Papa, is it tuberculosis?"

"Be quiet now, Marisia," Papa said. With his thick fingers he untangled Katrina's curls.

If Papa won't answer me, Marisia thought, it's true that Katrina has the disease Mr. Ciorka had. She remembered how Mr. Ciorka, in his last days, coughed into a blood-spattered handkerchief and how, when he tried to breathe, he pulled at the air with his pursed mouth as if he were sucking up water in droplets. The day after he died, she'd been taken into his room. She'd been careful not to look in the mirror that hung there, for Grandma had once told her that if you look into the mirror in the room where a dead person rests, someone else would die. She had been Katrina's own age then. She'd listened to the steady sound of people's praying, watching all the while to make sure no one approached the mirror. Nobody had.

"Marisia, are you all right?"

After his death Mrs. Ciorka had lost pounds and pounds and pounds.

"Marisia. Sit," she heard Mama say. "Look, she's gone pale."

By Easter, when she'd gone with Mama to bring Mrs. Ciorka a basket with colored Easter eggs and cakes and the Paschal lamb Mama made of butter and cheese and horseradish, the once-fat Mrs. Ciorka was skinny.

"You look as if you've gone a thousand miles away." Mama was pushing her down onto the bench. "Don't you faint on us now. Sit."

Marisia looked up. Katrina was butting against Papa's thigh with her head like a little goat. Beside her, Adam wiggled his fingers nervously, and beside Adam, Stefan ruffled his hair. "They can't mean it, sending us back," he said furiously "We'll all return then?"

Papa's words creaked when he talked. "I didn't bring my family all the way across the ocean just to take them back again. Stefan, you can't. It would mean your life. You have to go on."

"What about you, Papa?" Stefan asked.

"If Katrina and Mama were caught returning to

Lutrek, they'd land in prison. That's what'd happen, but Hamburg is safe." Slowly Papa stroked Katrina's back. "I'll go with them. I'll find work of some kind there. Mama, she'll take care of Katrina. We'll find a place to live. We'll get by."

"Marisia once had a cough and a fever so high that for days she made no sense at all," Mama said. "You talked like a mad person, Marisia. I cured you. I can make Katrina well. We'll come straight back here on another boat."

Marisia didn't know whether to believe Mama's words. She didn't know if Mama believed them herself.

"The boat returns the day after tomorrow," Papa told them. "Until then we'll all stay here. We'll stay together. And you, Marisia—you've got to make your decision."

"*My* decision?"

"You're fourteen years of age now." Papa hesitated, staring at her intently.

Was he too remembering her birthday? That was the night before they'd boarded the train to Hamburg. They'd camped near a stream with water that was as cold as ice, under stars that looked like pieces of ice tucked into the black German sky. That night Mama had sung a lullaby to her, the same one she had sung when Marisia was a baby.

"Adam has to come back with us," Papa said now, "but you can go with Stefan if you want. Come with us or go with him. You are old enough to decide for yourself now."

"But I don't know, Papa!"

Mama grabbed Marisia's hand. She grimaced at Papa.

"This is what I told you, Jozef. She's too young to make up her mind. Tell her that she can't leave us."

"Maria! We didn't come all this way to give up. I won't tell her she can't go with Stefan. You mustn't argue with me about this."

Mama shook out her red scarf and folded it in a square. She smoothed each wrinkle so carefully it seemed that she was thinking of nothing but that. Suddenly there were tears on her face.

"No more talk. Not now," Papa said. He brushed the side of Katrina's cheek with his mouth. "Come. They said we'll stay in their dormitory rooms tonight."

In the baggage area, Stefan swung a great bundle onto his shoulder. "Stefan," Marisia said, "I can't believe this is happening. It can't be happening. I have to tell Sofia somehow. I have to find her."

"I'll help you look for her," he said. "Let's store our things first."

Ahead of them, Katrina wrapped her legs and arms around Papa and gazed back at them over his shoulder.

Adam struggled along after Stefan, trying to hold a bundle as large as his. He tried to match Stefan's manly stride too, but he tottered when he did, just as a boy would.

Sofia looked from Stefan to Marisia. "Why are you crying? What's wrong?" she murmured.

From a distance Sofia's father called her name, and when Sofia turned, he rolled his heavy head at her like a great black bear. "Your father doesn't want to see you talking to me," Marisia said.

"Wait just a minute. I promise I'll come back."

Marisia watched Sofia cross the floor. Her walk was balanced and steady. Someone had taught Sofia to walk gracefully, Marisia guessed, just as they'd taught her French and music. How odd to be taught absolutely everything, like some circus animal made to perform tricks.

She brushed stray pieces of lint from Stefan's tattered tan jacket and said, "Stefan, go with her. Please. I can't go. Her father hates me."

"Why should he hate you? What are you talking about?"

"I can't explain now. Go and tell them everything. You must."

Impatiently Marisia watched Sofia and Stefan talk to Mr. Cybulski, and while she watched, she scratched at fleabites she had gotten on the ship. She rocked from her left foot to her right and back again. More minutes passed. What were they saying?

At last Sofia whirled around. She ran toward Marisia, grabbed her hands, and in her breathy voice said, "If you do come to America, you can come to my uncle's house and live there! We'd live together!"

"Your father said that?"

"I told him you helped Casimir that day on the lifeboat,

and Stefan promised him that you would never have taken him up there to play. Father says Mother said the same thing to him and he'll believe us. But Marisia..." Sofia fell silent. "I mean," she said after a moment, "if you come, it will be to work in the household. We were supposed to hire a maid because my aunt was worried about the extra chores our staying there would create. It was part of the bargain my father made with my aunt and uncle."

"Oh...oh, I see."

"But you'll come! You have to come!"

"You'll be the lady of the house and I'll be the servant."

"No, not to me. Don't say that. Marisia, don't. Just come!"

"I don't know what I'll do. Mama doesn't want me to go with Stefan, and how can I leave her when Katrina's so ill?"

That night Marisia, Mama, and Katrina slept in one room with the women. Papa, Stefan, and Adam slept in another with the men. When the lights were turned off, Marisia stared into the darkness. Her hair smelled of soap, which a woman had rubbed into her scalp in the showers, pressing so hard with her prickly fingers that Marisia longed to scream. Stefan claimed they used the stuff to kill lice and that they made everyone who slept here wash with it.

Marisia dozed but woke a minute later. Between rows of tiered bunk beds paced a woman who'd wrapped a blanket around her whole body. It dragged behind her.

Why was she awake? Had she been told she couldn't go on, that America didn't want her, either? Someone cried out in a dream.

At last daylight edged its way into the room, and Marisia sat up. Quietly, so as not to wake anyone, she pulled on her dress, slipping her arms into the sleeves. When she pulled up the blanket Katrina had kicked aside, Katrina kicked it away again in her sleep. Her cheeks were flushed, and her curls tumbled across the thin mattress. In the bunk above her, Mama slept, a faint whistle of air coming from her half-open mouth.

In the outside corridor, on a bench by a window, Marisia knelt. She looked out at the gray water, her square chin resting on her folded arms. She could feel the muscles all along them tighten up if she made fists. She wished her arms didn't pop with muscles like this, like a boy's arms.

For long minutes Marisia studied the choppy waves. This water led back to Germany and Poland. In Lutrek the birds would be returning after their winter's migration—the storks, the cuckoos and lapwings, the nightingales and larks. They'd perch in the willows by the stream, call out, fling themselves into the air when startled, glide over the trees. She wished she could see them, wished she could hear their singing.

What she did hear were footsteps. Marisia turned. Stefan walked toward her. "I woke up. I couldn't get back to sleep," he said when he reached her.

"I hardly slept at all. I don't know what to do. I wish this had never happened. I wish we'd never left."

Marisia knew she was whining like a child, but she felt too tired to care. "If you'd stayed in the army," she burst out, "we wouldn't be here at all. We wouldn't have run away from Poland. I never would have dreamed about America. I wouldn't have given it a thought."

She saw Stefan's face darken and expected him to shout at her. *Let him,* she said to herself. *It's true what I said.*

"I had to do what I did, Marisia."

"You didn't have to desert. Other boys go into the army and stay there." A boat bobbed up and down in the water, so far away that it was no bigger than her hand.

"You know why I deserted? I'll tell you. I don't talk about it, but I'll tell you. One night they put a friend of mine on special duty, a Polish soldier like me, Jerzy. After he came back, he looked terrible. I thought he was sick.

"Marisia, look at me now, not out that window! Sit down and look at me." Stefan was silent until she did. His eyebrows were puckered. "Days later Jerzy told me what he'd done. He said he couldn't live with himself any longer. This special duty they took him on — it was a firing squad. In the village they held a prisoner. She'd been a teacher in the village school. Do you know what her crime was? She'd taught her students in Polish, not in Russian as the czar ordered. Someone informed on her."

At the end of the hallway an old man tottered toward them, supporting his weight with a cane. He stopped, looked their way, and turned back the way he'd come, as if he didn't want to hear this story. Marisia didn't know if she wanted to hear it, either.

"Jerzy said they tied the woman to a post. One of the czar's officers told him that if he didn't fire, he'd be tied to the post, too. So he shot her. He said she'd screamed at them not to shoot. She pleaded. After that, he dreamt about her. He couldn't stop thinking about her. The day after he told me the story, I ran away." Marisia couldn't look at Stefan anymore. She looked down into her lap and clasped her right hand with her left.

"Marisia," Stefan said, "I tell you, it could have been me they ordered to do that. I couldn't stay after that. Would you stay? Just tell me. Would you?"

"No."

"Jerzy told me not to talk about it. Not ever. He didn't want anyone to know that Polish soldiers went and murdered a Polish girl because the Russians told them to. So I didn't say anything before. Don't tell even Papa or Mama. Don't tell anyone."

"I won't," Marisia promised.

"Sometimes I feel that it's my fault the family left." Stefan arched his back against the hard wall and stretched his long legs out, rotating them in one direction and then in the other. He never could stay still. He always shifted this way and that, Marisia realized.

"But if it is my fault, I don't care. I don't care. I can't live under the Russian czar. They've taken our land. They want to own us, too. You can't speak your own language, you can't..." Stefan's voice trailed off. He pulled his legs up and drummed furiously on his knees with the flat of his hands. "You shouldn't go back. Don't do it."

Marisia said, "Part of me wants to stay in America,

but part of me hates it here—all these people bossing us around, these men in their uniforms. When I say the English words I know, they can't even understand me."

"Say you did go back, Marisia. One day you'd marry and have children. They wouldn't be safe. You know how Aleksander died when he went off to war, our own brother? In the army the officers put him at the very front in a battle, along with all the other Poles. The Russian soldiers used the Poles like a shield. They fought behind them so they wouldn't get a bullet in their own heads. Papa found that out."

Marisia stared at two tan drips under the freshly painted wall across the aisle. She could smell the paint, a bitter, pinching smell, a smell that seemed like an echo of Stefan's story about Aleksander. "I can't really remember Aleksander," she said. "I only remember Mama's crying so much that afternoon, after we heard he'd been killed. It was during that big snowstorm. Remember? Papa had to climb out the windows to get to the cowshed because the door wouldn't open with all the snow piled around it."

She remembered how the house groaned so loudly in the ferocious winds that it seemed to be sobbing, the way Mama kept sobbing all that day. If she went back, she would be choosing to live Mama's nightmare all over again.

"God help me," Marisia said. "I can't return. I'll stay with you."

Mama cast her eyes down. "Papa said you must decide, but I say you're too young to do this."

"She'll be safe with Sofia's family, Maria," Papa told Mama. "You don't need to worry."

"So many things could happen, Jozef! Here you let your own daughter go into a strange country by herself!"

"We agreed," Papa said loudly, "that she would decide."

Mama cried out, "I didn't think she'd decide to leave her family! All along I thought she'd decide to return with us."

"Stefan is her family, too. Besides, I won't have her give up hope. I won't have it!"

Marisia felt torn in half by their arguing.

A half-dozen times in the morning Marisia decided to tell Mama that she'd changed her mind. A half-dozen times in the afternoon she wanted to tell Papa that America wasn't a good place for a girl.

Instead she filled out immigration forms, which Papa signed for her. She refolded her clothes and tied the quilt that held them into a tight bundle. She cut out paper dolls for Katrina from a newspaper they'd found. She listened to Adam when he told her he'd seen a crazy woman and to Papa when he told her she would learn English in the American night schools. She went with Stefan to change their money into American dollars and promised Mama she'd do all Sofia's mother told her to do.

It was a relief when the day was finally over and the lights went out in the dormitory room. Tomorrow Mama, Papa, Adam, and Katrina would board the ship that was making its return voyage, but Marisia told herself that she would not think of that.

To escape her thoughts Marisia pulled her blankets up around her head and burrowed under them, her knees drawn up, her back curled into a down-turned crescent. In the cave she made, her breath felt hot. When she was Katrina's age and frightened by the whirling noise of a bat that had come into the house or the rustling of a ghost at the window—which Mama said was not a ghost at all and don't be silly—she'd huddled under her covers just like this.

Hours later, Marisia tossed the covers back. A rising half-moon had lodged at the bottom corner of the high windows. Marisia watched the orb of weak light it cast on the glass. The moon did not move for such a long, long time that Marisia fancied it had become stuck there and couldn't. She willed it to stay exactly where it had settled and go no higher in the black sky. If the moon were truly stuck, if the moon did not move, morning would never come.

CHAPTER SIX

TURNING SIDEWAYS on the brown upholstered seat that ran the length of the elevated train, Marisia leaned forward to stare out the window. Her nose touched the pane. On the stairs of a fire escape, so close to their clattering car that Marisia felt she could reach out and pull at her blue cotton dress, a woman ladled water out of a bucket. She threw it at two tiny children who wiggled with delight, the way Katrina would.

What was Katrina doing now? Was she holding on to the ship's railing and staring back at the land? Running along the deck and sliding on its wet surface? Tucking her doll into a bed she'd made for it from scrunched up blouses and petticoats?

Stefan nudged Marisia. "This is our stop," he said. The engineer leaned his head out and looked back at them as they stepped from the car. From the smokestack of the elevated, sparks flew up.

Clinging to the ironwork railing, Marisia followed

Stefan down the long staircase to the street, her bundle of belongings slung across her shoulder. At the bottom an enormous man with a gold tooth yelled some English words at Marisia, then threw his head back to let out a howl of laughter. Marisia felt her cheeks flush. Why was he laughing at her? Stefan called to Marisia to follow him, and she hurried after him along the tangle of streets east of the Bowery.

Crowding the sidewalks were pushcarts filled with shirts and fruit and fat loaves of bread and shopping bags and shoes, razors, soap, hot pretzels, baskets, scarves, thread, candles, pencils, notebooks, caps, and every other thing a person might need. In German and Yiddish and Russian and Polish, peddlers yelled, and they waved their wares at her.

Stefan pushed through the coming waves of people and carts with his long stride. A mud-colored horse, cran-ing its neck in the air, kicked at Stefan as he passed behind it. Stefan skittered out of the way.

At the next corner, over the crashing of metal wheels on cobblestones, Stefan yelled straight into Marisia's face in order to be heard. "Papa told me to search for a room around here. This street's called

Delancey. See where it says that on the sign there?" He pointed and Marisia nodded. "Now we've got to look for these words here," he added, tapping on the paper. In block letters, carefully printed in Papa's fine hand, were the English words *Room to Rent—Room to Let*. "If people take boarders, they put signs with these words on them in the windows."

Midway down the first block, a man smiled widely at Marisia and rubbed at his big stomach. "Girlie," he called in Russian, "you look worn out. Leave that bundle of yours here. I'll watch it for you. Come back in an hour, two hours, three, whatever you need." Without hesitating, Marisia let her heavy bundle down. The man's small daughter, her black hair a snarl of curls, grabbed it.

"Wait a minute," Stefan called to the girl. "Hey, leave it!" he yelled, following her when she stepped behind their cart.

"I'm moving it out of the way, is all." The girl wiped her forehead with the back of a grubby hand.

"We'll keep our things with us, Marisia," Stefan ordered. He seized the bundle back.

"He doesn't trust us," the girl said to her father.

"These newcomers are so suspicious. You try to give them a helping hand, they don't want it. Get along on your own, then," the man spat at Stefan in heavy Russian while the girl stared at him and gnawed a fingernail.

A few hundred feet farther on Stefan turned and said, "What if they'd stolen your things, those people?"

"They were only trying to help," Marisia grumbled.

She clutched her bundle when it began to slip off her shoulder.

"You can't just hand things over to anybody. Don't be so naive."

"I'm not naive!"

"Oh, excuse me. No one can fool you, then. You're a woman of the world, a perfect judge of human character. That man was an upstanding citizen. We can be sure of that."

"Stop it. Leave me alone." Angrily she followed Stefan. "I know as much about the world as you do," she muttered loudly. He didn't look back, and she didn't know if he'd heard her.

For more than two hours they searched for a place for Stefan, but all the rooms they inspected on Delancey, Orchard, Rivington, and Suffolk streets were cramped and dark and crowded. In one, water had to be carried in buckets from a backyard pump up five flights of stairs. In another, a thin Jewish woman struggled to boil a kettle of water on a broken coal stove that leaked smoke at every joint. Her kitchen table was no more than three boards propped up on wooden crates. Five of her children ran in and out of the room in a game of tag, screeching and giggling.

Fourteen people lived in another flat. Stefan was told he could sleep at night on the dining room table. Marisia thought the skinny man who talked to Stefan about the rent looked like a rodent because he had a small, sharp face and a pointed nose that twitched above his pencil-thin mustache.

"We have a mat we lay across the table," the man boomed out, as if announcing a grand event. His voice was bigger than he was. "It's comfortable enough for a young man like yourself. The last fellow liked it well enough. Only four and a half dollars a month, see? Costs you next to nothing. That way you'll save all your wages. That way you'll be rich before you know it."

"No," Stefan said tiredly. "It's not what I want." They walked down a dim staircase, where the air had long ago gone stale. Near the bottom, blocking the stairs, two children sat together, looking not like humans at all but like two small piles of rags.

"Four dollars, then!" the man shouted as Stefan squeezed his way past the children.

Outside, Marisia blinked at the brightness. Here the air smelled of manure the horses dropped and of spilt, sour milk. On fire escapes that spiraled up the sides of buildings, clothes, hung out to dry, snapped up and down in the wind. Up there, too, far over her head, smoke wriggled from dozens of chimneys and left smudges all across the blue April sky. In the streets people shoved and rushed. Marisia wanted to cover her ears against the noise they made.

"You're tired," Stefan said. "Stay here. There's another room five or six doors down the street. I'll go look at that. Stay here and rest for a couple of minutes." He left Marisia where she stood on the stoop. A passing woman smiled at her; another frowned. Nearby an old peddler sold crushed lemon ice to a ruddy-cheeked man who flipped him a copper penny. In mid-air, the peddler grasped it with one hand, stroking fitfully at his long beard with the other.

Marisia licked her parched lips, then took out a coin from her cotton purse. The peddler straightened his vest with its torn buttonholes and watched her approach. Taking her coin, he grinned at Marisia. He had large yellowing teeth, like the teeth of a horse, and all of a sudden, like a horse, he gave a neighing bellow. In that instant she felt a pull from behind. "Hey, there," the peddler yelled.

Marisia bellowed herself and whirled. A boy scuttled out of her reach, her purse in his grimy hand, his shirt-tail flying behind. A woman sitting on a straw stool, a big clump of greens in her hand, waved the greens in the air and shouted encouragement as Marisia pulled up her skirts and bounded forward.

The boy dodged between two horse-drawn carts. Looking back wildly over his shoulder, he scrambled past a cigar store's wooden Indian and jumped over the legs of a man who leaned against a wall, a crutch in his lap. Next he darted across the street right under the bobbing nose of a horse that pulled a delivery wagon. The driver, yanking back with all his might on the reins, cursed.

For a desperate minute the wagon, piled high with crates and sacks and barrels, concealed the boy from Marisia's sight. In the middle of the street she stood stock-still, not knowing where he'd gone. A small boy holding a basket of black-and-white puppies pulled on her skirt. "Puppies, see 'em? Want one?" Slowly, ever so slowly, the wagon creaked by. Marisia pulled away from the child's grasp.

Heart racing, she ran past children playing stickball at the edge of an alley. At the corner, Marisia stopped. She jerked her head to the right, but didn't see the thief. She looked to the left. A small figure—it could be the boy—scampered past a woman carrying a big straw basket. Marisia jostled people out of her way along this new street, and there the boy was in plain view. He trotted along, elbows bouncing.

Only occasionally did he look back. Apparently he thought he'd lost her.

Marisia came closer and closer, so close she could see the worn-down heels on the boy's shoes and his bristly hair. When she made a grab for him, he staggered. Her hand on his shoulder, she pushed with all her might so that he fell in a heap in front of her. He yelped. Her knee scraped on the rough pavement as she threw herself on top of him.

"It's mine," she gasped and wrenched at the purse. The boy closed his fist and pulled back.

Sprawled out under her, babbling words she didn't know, he looked frightened. Marisia pulled at his short mustard-colored hair. "Give it to me!" She pulled harder. The boy's eyes filled with pain.

Suddenly, he tossed his head and bit her hand, the teeth sinking straight down to the bone. Marisia screamed in pain. Dust caught in her throat. Enraged, she bounced twice on the boy's stomach as hard as she could, aware that he was smaller than she was but not caring, aware she might be hurting him and not caring. The air went out of the boy. His body collapsing, he opened his fist. The purse dropped to the ground. He panted in short, hard breaths now and turned his face away from her. Streaks of dirt covered his cheek and neck.

Still sitting on him, her legs akimbo, Marisia opened the purse to count her money. Hearing laughter, she looked up to see a small circle of people around her. One man clapped and others joined in. Startled, she held her bloody hand to her mouth and stared about her. A young woman with a bright blue skirt pulled Marisia up and dusted her off with broad swipes of her hand.

Uncertainly, slowly, the boy got to his feet. Two buttons were missing on his torn, filthy shirt. His body was slight, his knees knobby and scraped. His thin chest heaved. All of a sudden a bull-necked man stepped forward from the circle and slapped him across the face. The boy fell back. Laughing, someone caught him and pushed him toward the man who'd hit him. Tears were on the boy's face now, along with a bruising red mark that the big man's hand had made.

When the bull-necked man raised his hand a second time, Marisia grabbed his arm. "No, don't! Don't hit him. Don't do it." The man stared, not understanding Marisia's words, but he let his arm drop because he understood her meaning well enough.

"Why not?" A staunch woman yelled out. "He stole your purse, didn't he?"

"Yes, but—"

The man who'd slapped the boy interrupted to say

something to Marisia in German, then made a grab for the boy and pulled him through the crowd.

At the corner they turned. They were gone. Marisia watched that empty corner, confused. In the eyes of the onlookers, she'd won, but inside of herself she felt she'd lost somehow.

"Don't you worry now," the woman in the blue skirt said to Marisia in Polish. "If nobody catches these boys, then they're only headed for worse trouble. That's a fact. You find children with no parents at all sleeping on hay barges on the river, eating nothing fit for humans. Half of 'em grow up with nothing at all, and they turn to thieving." With these words the woman wiped at the bloody teeth marks the boy had left on Marisia's hand. "You're fresh into America, aren't you?"

"What will they do with him?"

"Maybe one thing, maybe another," the woman said with a shrug. It was an answer that wasn't any answer at all. "It's not your worry now, is it?"

"I don't know."

"I say it's not."

"Will they put him in jail?"

"Don't you go thinking any more about it. There's a good girl."

"But..."

"There's nothing you can do now. I'll tell you that," the woman said in a firm voice, her hands on her hips.

"Stefan, my brother, he'll be looking for me," Marisia said. "We've been searching all day for a place for him to live."

When Marisia turned, a broad-faced, bearded man bowed in her direction. "This one will make it in America," he called in Polish to the woman at Marisia's side. "She's got the nerve it takes! She's a fighter, all right."

"Mr. Pulaski," the woman called back, "that little room you talked about yesterday, the one your two cousins were living in. What's happening with it? This girl's brother, he needs a place, she says. You'll see," the woman murmured to Marisia, pulling her toward Mr. Pulaski, who stood grinning at them. "Mr. Pulaski's a barber, and he can afford a better place than most you're going to see. Won't keep a dozen people in it like some of them, either. He rents out the one room and sleeps in the parlor himself."

Yes, Mr. Pulaski would be glad to show the room to Marisia and any brother of hers. It would be an honor. He tipped his derby hat like a gentleman, though the patches at the elbows of his gray striped jacket showed that he could hardly be called one.

The room on Ludlow Street, like Mr. Pulaski himself, made all it could out of the little it had. Through a clean window soft light fell on a scrubbed floor. "It's decent enough," Stefan said to Marisia.

In a tiny mirror over the dresser, Mr. Pulaski adjusted his shiny black bow tie and smoothed the lapels of his jacket. "I've been here more than ten years, but I remember what it was like my very first day in America as if it were yesterday. The first day is not the easiest day, is it?

You're just another dirty immigrant off the boat, a green-horn, and everybody wants to take advantage of you. That's it, am I right?" He turned to face them. "You haven't had a proper bath in weeks. You can't speak a word of the English they're talking at you. Can't understand the Yiddish either or the Italian or any of it. You've looked at rooms that aren't fit for a dog. There's the noise, the smells. Out there on these streets there's more people than you knew God ever had time to make. It's true, isn't it?"

Not waiting for a reply, Mr. Pulaski smiled broadly and slapped Stefan on the shoulder. "You'll manage, though. Just follow your sister's lead," he said, nodding toward Marisia.

Stefan shuffled his feet while Marisia laughed out loud.

In the kitchen that night Mr. Pulaski set a big tin tub near the coal stove, filled it halfway with buckets of water from the sink, and threw in two kettles of boiling water to take off the chill. "There now. You can have the first bath and when you're done, Stefan will get his turn."

Left alone in the little kitchen, Marisia undressed and stepped into the bath. She leaned back against the tub's hard edge. Today there'd been too many new sights and smells, too much noise, hundreds of tall buildings and dozens of unfamiliar streets and thousands of strangers. There'd been the scrawny boy who'd taken her purse too. Where was he now? She cupped water in her hand. It dribbled over the sides and leaked between her fingers. Had she hurt him when she'd pounced on him?

Was there anyone to help him? Why did she feel guilty when he was the thief?

Papa might know the answers to these questions. Mama might know. They were not here.

The kitchen was thankfully quiet. There was only the thin hiss of a gas lamp in the corner and muffled sounds that came from far away— too far away to matter at all, Marisia told herself. Only her own thoughts could disturb her now. She closed her eyes and sank down into the water, all the way up to her chin.

Waking, Marisia stretched. She listened to morning noises—the rattling of a pot in the kitchen and the howling of a cat on the floor above. From somewhere—it seemed as if from a rooftop nearby—came a prayerful chanting in a singsong voice. She turned and watched her brother, who still slept on top of the quilt he'd folded double on the floor for a mat. "Stefan," she whispered. "It's time to get up."

He stirred and glared. He groaned out, "Don't wake me when I'm sound asleep." Then Stefan sat up with a jolt. "We're in America." At his own announcement, he shook himself awake. He smoothed his unruly hair and rose.

An hour later Stefan and Marisia had left the rambling streets of the Lower East Side behind and were traveling uptown on the elevated train to find Sofia's address on Ninety-third Street east of Lexington Avenue. This new neighborhood was like another world. Gone were the carts, the stench of refuse, the rag pickers, the gangs of children, the barking dogs, the fire escapes, and the lines of laundry. Marisia stared at a passing motor car. Inside it a man sat upright, a plaid scarf wrapped around his neck, a visor covering his eyes.

Before Sofia's house, Marisia hesitated. She checked the number she saw on the door against the number on the paper she held in her hand. "Come on," Stefan urged. "We're here. What are you waiting for?"

At the ringing of the bell, feet thumped inside the house. The woman who answered the door was all bones, like a child's drawing of a stick figure. Her mouth was a thin horizontal line; her nose, a thin vertical one.

"I am Miss Bolinski, Marisia Bolinski," Marisia said in careful, slow English, trying out the phrase she'd practiced. In her mouth the strange words were as uncomfortable as pebbles. "Sofia is...Sofia is on the boat...I come to her house," she hesitated. "Please, you speak Polish? Please, you speak Russian?"

"Yes, miss, we all speak Polish in this household."

With relief Marisia said, "I met Sofia Cybulski on the boat to America, and it was arranged that I should come here." The woman only stared at Marisia with narrowed eyes. "I'll be a maid in the household, they told me," Marisia went on.

"Oh, it's you, then. They said you'd come, but I didn't think it would be today. Well, I can use help. It's about time. This household is too big for one maid. They expect me to do everything. Come in, then, and what did you say your name is? Who's this with you? They said nothing about any man."

"My brother, Stefan."

"What's he doing here?" On the maid's nose and cheeks were irritated patches of red, as if someone had scrubbed her too hard with a rough washcloth.

All of a sudden behind the maid's back Sofia appeared. With a cry she ran and threw her arms around Marisia. The maid raised scrawny eyebrows in disapproval. She clucked her tongue. Sofia whispered in Marisia's ear, "Don't pay any attention to Magdalena. She looks at everybody like that."

Calling good-bye, Stefan trotted down the stairs.

By nightfall Marisia had scoured pots, dusted the lampshades in the hushed parlor, changed Casimir's bedding and Sofia's, cleaned the kitchen floor, beat the dust from an oriental rug that she could barely carry outside, polished the front windows, scrubbed carrots and potatoes, and watered the tall indoor plants in their giant pots. In the kitchen, after dinner, she wiped at a water glass with a dishtowel.

As she'd done a dozen times that day, Magdalena pinched Marisia on the arm. "There's a spot! There! Can't you see it?" Her low forehead was creased with worried lines. "That's the good crystal. You must do it the right way or you're no use to me at all."

In the small room she was given at the head of the stairs, Marisia could hear the footfalls of all who passed up and down. If she stood on her tiptoes, she could see out the little oval window, where trees swayed and stars littered the sky. The sky reached all the way to Poland. In

Poland it was said that you could ask the stars any question. If you then listened with all your heart, you would hear an answer more true than any human answer. She'd been told this as a child. She'd told this to Katrina.

The sleeves of her nightgown fell back. Along her arms were tiny bruises from Magdalena's sharp, disapproving fingers. She rubbed at the marks, but rubbing wasn't going to erase them, she knew. If she did everything correctly tomorrow, she wondered, would Magdalena leave her alone?

No answer came from the stars.

After another minute at the window, yawning for the third time, Marisia turned away. She blew out the lamp and slipped into the bed.

The moment she closed her eyes, Marisia saw Mama's hollyhocks rearing up toward the sky all along the birch bark fence in Lutrek. She opened her eyes and stared into the darkness. When she closed her eyes a second time, their cow appeared with broad milklike splashes of white along her black sides. Then Marisia saw furrows, their edges crumpling in the heat of the sun. Papa dropped seeds into them. His back was bent, his cap pulled low. Mama appeared in a blouse embroidered with cross-stitching. She was setting wooden plates out on a table, preparing a celebration. Somehow Marisia knew the celebration was for Grandma because it was Grandma's name day, Saint Ursula's Day.

Again, turning in the bed, she closed her eyes and again she was back home. This time Grandma stood before her, a black shawl draped around her shoulders.

Grandma turned to light a fire in the hearth. She blessed the flames that rose up, as one should. In the dark, eyes closed, Marisia could see how brightly Grandma's fire burned. Drowsy, she even felt its warmth.

Was this fire the star's answer to some question she hadn't had the sense to ask?

"Why do you do that?" Marisia pushed Magdalena's pinching fingers off her. It was her fourth day in the household.

"Don't you talk back to me or you'll be out of here in a minute. You must learn to do things properly. If you don't, it's me the missus will blame. I'll have you do things right or you'll leave. And then where will you go? You'll not have a morsel to put in your mouth if you leave a good position." The words shot out like sparks.

Marisia stared at Magdalena's gaunt face. In it the small eyes were hot.

"Off you'd go to the tenements. You know what happens to girls in the tenements? They work until they drop. You see them begging in the streets, girls half your age. Begging or worse, it's shameful — I can't even tell you what!"

Without saying a word to Magdalena, Marisia lowered her head and turned to her next chore. What would Papa say now? "Be patient," he would tell her.

The silverware rattled noisily as Marisia threw it into the drawer.

Mama would give a little speech. "What do you

expect? That life will be easy? That's only another one of your daydreams, Marisia."

Maybe Mama would say that, but Mama wouldn't like Magdalena any more than she herself did.

In the following weeks, whenever she could, Marisia escaped with Sofia to the garden or the back steps or the dark front parlor and then she was happy. One day they shared a banana with Casimir, a food none of them had ever had before. Another day, Marisia put on Sofia's black stockings, which were embroidered with flowers and which Sofia said were much in fashion. When Sofia insisted that she try on the satin evening shoes with their jet-black beads, Marisia had worn them, too. Because they were too big, she'd tottered and tripped her way along the upstairs corridor, making Sofia laugh. She'd laughed so hard herself that she could barely walk.

Every time they met, no matter where they were, Sofia drilled English words and sentences into Marisia's head. Often Marisia couldn't wait for these lessons, but at other times she might say, "I'm too tired to care about English, Sofia. Please, no more words right now."

One evening she said that when her back ached from pumping water from cisterns in the cellar to water tanks on the floors above. She sat beside Sofia in the front parlor on the dark horsehair sofa while Sofia straightened the collar of Marisia's blouse and smoothed her wrinkled skirt. Next to her own chafed hands, Sofia's were creamy white. Irritably Marisia pushed those fine hands away. "Quit trying to make me perfect, Sofia. It's no use. I'm the maid, remember?"

Sofia was still. In the hallway a clock ticked.

"Yesterday I asked Father if Mr. Gregory could tutor you when he gives me my lessons. And you know what he said? It would give you airs above your station." As always there were pauses between Sofia's words, like sad, little holes in the sentences she made. As always, her eyelids seemed to quiver, the way mice quivered at a footfall, the way moths quivered at a window.

Marisia said, "If you teach me, then you'll be the one to give me airs above my station."

"They want me to have airs. They insist. If I have them, you must have them too."

"You're disobeying your father, you know."

Sofia shook her head. "You have to try. Just a little more," she urged, "and say the words the way I do. The accent is important. It makes all the difference. People look down on you, Mr. Gregory says, unless you speak the way they speak in the upper classes. From the way you say the words people can tell if you're the servant or if you're the lady."

On the ship, Marisia recalled, there'd been a lady in first class who tilted her head carefully to one side and back again as if that head were not a head at all but rather a precious crown. She'd studied that woman intently. She'd studied her so that in America—where anything was possible, everybody said—she might be like her, so that she might raise a teacup ever so slowly to her own lips and arch an eyebrow and give a leisurely, deliberate nod to someone in a room.

Marisia took Sofia's hand, the hand she'd shoved aside

a moment before. She ran a thumb along Sofia's clear nails and listened to the words she spoke. Carefully she said each one after her.

The weeks in the house turned into months. Spring became summer. Except for the fact that the temperature rose to an unbearable heat by mid-afternoon, little changed in the daily routines that Marisia followed, routines that were set out like law. On Sundays, according to that routine, Marisia was allowed a half-day off and she fled from the house as soon as Stefan came to take her out.

One day early in September Stefan reported that he'd met someone who hired men to work in the train yards by the Hudson River. "Packing olives, it's only the start. I promise you I'm headed for better. You'll see. I'll get one of these other jobs I've been asking about. Maybe in the train yards."

Stefan cracked peanuts out of their shell and threw them into the air, flipping his head back to catch them. One flew right past him and bounced along the ground. "I won't come home smelling of olives and brine for all of my life," he said. He straightened his back and adjusted the hard, round collar on his new shirt.

Dressed in black and white, a nanny passed with a squalling baby in its carriage. A policeman in a helmet regarded them solemnly, a nightstick tucked under his arm, a copper badge on his chest.

"When I learn more English," Marisia announced, wanting to match Stefan's claim, "maybe I'll be able to get some other position. I already know hundreds of words and sentences." *And I know how to say them the way a lady should,* she wanted to add, but she knew that Stefan would mock her if she did.

They turned toward the East River and entered a churchyard surrounded by a cast iron railing. In it were pretty benches. "I wish I could come here every day," Marisia said. "All summer long they've let me out only when you come. Magdalena

doesn't trust me out alone. I don't know what she thinks I'll do—run away or what."

In a rising wind, the leaves on a poplar spun in circles. A newspaper left on a bench flew up in all directions.

"I should take you back," Stefan said.

"No, not yet."

In the house, Magdalena would be rushing about to slam all the windows tight against this same gust. Marisia didn't want to return to that shut-up house. Here, overhead, the sunlight loped across the top branches of the trees and small birds flapped in windswept lines. Marisia picked up a leaf that had changed from green to toasted bronze. When would her life change—and how?

CHAPTER SEVEN

MAGDALENA CHOPPED NUTS into fine pieces for the topping of a cake, her knife moving so fast it blurred. "What does Mr. Finley look like?" Marisia asked her.

"He looks like the sort of person Mr. Cybulski would invite into this house to visit, of course. He looks like a proper gentleman."

"Is he handsome?"

Magdalena's little dark eyes only clicked shut in answer. "Now take the teacups in. Leave the cups by the tea service, and come back for the cake. Mind your manners. Don't stare at the gentleman. It's not your business to inspect the company, I'm sure. And don't dawdle."

When Marisia entered the parlor, Sofia was seated at the piano bench, her white muslin dress touching the floor, her black hair streaming down her back. Dutifully she played a Mozart piece, one that Marisia knew she loved and always played with spirit, fingers flying. Why did her fingers now pass so mechanically across those black and white keys, as if she were practicing scales?

As soon as she spied Mr. Finley, Marisia knew the answer to her question. She started. She couldn't help it. Teacups clanked loudly on her tray. At the sound, Mr. Finley clutched the arm of the brocade settee that he sat on. Marisia saw how his neck rose in swelling pink pleats above his white collar and how his eyes bulged out as if that collar were choking him. Circling the bald spot on the top of his head, like a shabby halo, were thin wisps of blond hair. He glanced at Sofia, then looked down at his own knees, which he studied with far more interest that he'd shown Sofia.

"Mr. Finley must be twice your age!" Marisia sputtered.

"More than that," Sofia said. "He's thirty-seven. His first wife died a year ago."

"Of boredom, I'll bet you anything."

Sofia leaned back on the garden bench and pulled all the petals off a yellow rose. "His father died unexpectedly three years ago, leaving him a fortune from a leather factory he'd just sold. Mr. Finley is on a supervising board for the transcontinental railroad and has money in mining in the West and more money in a land-irrigation scheme. Father says he is definitely a man who is going places." Sofia's voice was so blurred she seemed to be talking with a hand pressed over her mouth.

Behind her, swarming bees made a monotonous humming sound as they hovered over the flowers. The sound felt as muggy as the day.

"We sat in that parlor for hours with him. We discussed his politics. He can't abide President Roosevelt, something about his labor reform plan, whatever that is. We discussed his allergies. He can't go near cats or dogs or flowers or grass. He had a great deal to say of the distress that it causes him. We discussed his diet. He does not eat out because restaurants are not healthy. He will not eat cabbage. He allows himself a brandy after dinner because he thinks one glass has medicinal value."

"Sofia, you can't marry him. You just can't."

Sofia ripped one rose petal into smaller and smaller pieces. "We talked on and on and on about him as if he were the very center of the universe." Her voice grew so faint that Marisia could barely hear her. "Father says that if I married him, I'd learn to like him. A woman has many years to learn to like the husband her parents choose. It's an acquired taste. It doesn't happen at once. He says I must understand all that."

"You won't ever like him, Sofia. He's lifeless. He's awful."

Sofia didn't answer. She didn't look up. She didn't stir.

"Sofia?"

Still she didn't answer. Sun covered her and small beads of sweat formed on her forehead. It looked to Marisia as if Sofia might simply melt there on her bench in the sun and that would be the end of her.

In a corner of the garden, the lion-colored cat Marisia had adopted stalked a small finch. Marisia picked a pebble from the ground and tossed it at the bird to make it fly into the air out of the cat's reach. At that, the cat, named Washington after the first president, turned and stared at Marisia without any emotion in his eyes, neither disturbed nor pleased by what she'd done. Marisia called his name, and Washington stalked toward her, taking his time, regal as a lord.

Marisia scooped the cat up and dumped him into Sofia's lap. This made Sofia stir at last. She reached out a finger and scratched at Washington's ears, which twitched back and forth.

Marisia said, "Stefan can walk from his flat to where the real President Washington lived. He sees everything—gypsy women and men from China and skyscrapers, and only last week he saw a fight. A man cut someone with a razor. There was blood everywhere, Stefan says."

"You sound too pleased about that blood," Sofia retorted, making a face. She ran Washington's fluffy tail through her fingers and said, "You wouldn't know he was the same cat, the scrawny thing you started feeding a month ago."

"If Magdalena ever finds out how many saucers of milk I've stolen out of the house for Washington, she'll toss me out into the streets the way she's always threatening to do. He climbs along the drainpipe now right up to my window. He meows to come in. He's sure it's his own home."

Washington hopped from Sofia's lap to Marisia's own.

"Home." Sofia scattered the rose petals to the ground and stood up. "Marriage and a home—it's what I wanted, and now... I thought Mr. Finley might not like me, but Father insists he will. His mother came from Poland, so my being Polish won't stand in the way. Father claims it's even a point in my favor. They don't want someone who's too American. They want an old-fashioned girl."

"Someone who's ready to obey. That's what they mean, Sofia."

Sofia wet her lips with her tongue. She stared in front of her. "I'm so thirsty. All day, I've felt so thirsty."

From the back porch Magdalena's shrill call for Marisia pierced the air, and Marisia said, "I'd better go."

"The perfect maid, my aunt says—Magdalena's the perfect maid. My aunt took her in after Magdalena's parents died in a smallpox epidemic. She was only four or five. My aunt brags that she's molded her into the maid anyone would want." Sofia clasped her hands together. "Twenty years from now I'll be the perfect Mrs. Finley, with no thoughts of my own, doing exactly as I'm told."

"No, you won't. Don't believe that, Sofia." Marisia pushed Washington into Sofia's arms. "Take him for me." She rose.

Washington snuggled under Sofia's chin. Marisia stopped dead in her tracks. "You said he has allergies."

"Mr. Finley?"

"Allergies to cats," Marisia said.

"Yes."

"To cats, to flowers, to...what else? Never mind! Did you go near him at all today, Sofia?"

"I stayed as far away from him as I could."

"When is he coming again?"

"Saturday, for high tea. Why? What does it matter?" Sofia demanded.

"Sofia, we can weave cat hair in your hair. We'll stuff rose petals in your dress. You'll sit close by him. He'll think he's allergic to you."

Magdalena's call came again.

"It could never work, a plan like that!"

"It will!" Marisia insisted. "He won't want you!"

When Marisia reached the porch, Magdalena gave her a stinging slap. "When I was your age, I ran at the call of my mistress as if my life depended on it!" Her small frame huffed up with pride.

Mr. Finley's eyes were puffy and suspicious. He backed away from Sofia when she leaned toward him to say good-bye. He sneezed.

"I am so sorry," Sofia's mother said, handing him his coat. "I can't imagine ..."

From behind curtains in the front parlor, Sofia and Marisia peeked out at Mr. Finley, who put on goggles and wrapped a green driving coat around himself. "He looks like a fat green beetle," Marisia said. She saw how Mr. Finley's arms whirled in a frantic circle as he cranked the car to start it. "If you married him," she said, "you could drive in his motor car and wear goggles like those."

"And talk on a telephone. He has one."

At last the car sputtered and roared. When it pulled into the street, Sofia grabbed Marisia's hands and, balancing against Marisia's weight, turned around and around the room. They circled again. Marisia's skirt swirled out. Faster and faster they went. Sofia's hair tumbled from the pins that fastened it. The rose petals they'd stuffed into the bodice of her dress shook loose and floated into the air.

Too light-headed to stand straight, Marisia tipped sideways. "I'll fall over," she said, trying to slow down.

"Keep going! Faster!"

"I can't!"

Sofia's feet tapped crazily. "Remember on the boat when you said I was too good? I'm not too good anymore, am I?"

Marisia stared at the walls, which shifted dizzingly back and forth. Pictures rocked in their heavy, gold-colored frames. "No!" she laughed. "You've taught me English and I've taught you to be terrible. Now stop!"

Still Sofia spun her, laughing recklessly as she'd never laughed before.

The front door slammed shut. The spinning halted. Marisia shook her head and tried to bring things back into focus. She gripped the side of the sofa for balance and in that instant heard an angry voice. "So odd," Mr. Cybulski was shouting from the other side of the parlor door. "Decidedly odd. I don't like it one bit, not one bit."

Breathing hard, Marisia exchanged a sharp glance with Sofia, whose body stiffened. "He refused my invitation to come next week," Mr. Cybulski went on. "Said he'd be out of town. Of course it's this damnable sneezing of his. Something in the house makes him sneeze. Where is that girl?"

"Here, Father," Sofia called, crossing to the door and opening it.

Mr. Cybulski glowered.

"Albert, surely she cannot be blamed," Sofia's mother said, stepping to his side, and glancing at him with feverish, alarmed eyes. "She behaved entirely like a lady to Mr. Finley."

Sofia's father turned on his heel and stomped away with his rolling, bearlike gait.

Her mother took Sofia's hand. "It's not your fault, but your father is disappointed. Mr. Finley was all that he'd hoped for."

"And you, Mother? Is Mr. Finley all you'd hoped for?" Sofia asked.

Mrs. Cybulski put a hand to her pale throat. As if she were going to strangle herself, she tightened it. She didn't speak but gave a small shake of her head that could mean no—Marisia wasn't sure. She put one finger to her lips in warning. She led the girls away from the dark sitting room.

Through the kitchen window, while she scrubbed at piles of dishes, Marisia watched clouds skitter along the sky. Near the cherry tree Casimir dragged a stick for Washington, but he dropped it when Marisia waved to him. Waving back, he started running toward the house. The cat leapt onto the garden wall to bat at overhanging branches that tumbled from the fig tree in the next yard.

Fussing, Magdalena entered the kitchen through the swinging doors. Casimir followed right behind her. He plopped himself down on a kitchen chair and asked for bread and jam while Magdalena glared at Marisia, her face pinched up into furious wrinkles. "Why are there rose petals all over the front sitting room? There were no roses in there."

Marisia caught her breath. She ducked a teacup under the suds. Magdalena cackled on. "Rose petals! There must be two hundred of them on the floor. Is it you girls?"

"I didn't see any rose petals," Marisia said, quite honestly.

Broom and dustpan in her arms, Magdalena left the kitchen, almost at a run. Marisia dried her hands nervously and pressed her lips together. "What's wrong?" Casimir asked.

"Nothing. If Magdalena just keeps quiet, it'll be nothing at all."

"Quiet about what?"

"Shhhh." Marisia took a loaf of bread and cut a thick slice. On it she spooned strawberry jam. Casimir ate. Done, he wiped the jam off his lips with the back of his hand.

"Enough?" Marisia asked.

Casimir nodded and jiggled his feet. His eyes, like a puppy's, followed her every move.

It was not Magdalena who entered the kitchen next, but Sofia's father. In his fleshy fist were rose petals. "What are these?"

Behind Mr. Cybulski the kitchen doors swung open a third time. Sofia stood there, her eyes on her father, her face as white as her dress, her eyes in that white face a startling blue.

Mr. Cybulski brought his flushed face to within an inch of Marisia's. Instantly she recoiled, as she would recoil from burning heat. When Marisia took a step backwards, Mr. Cybulski stepped forward and shook his fist, bellowing, "What are these? He couldn't stop sneezing, isn't that right? He's allergic to flowers. You put Sofia up to this."

"Father, don't! It was me, not her. I did it, not Marisia."

At her words, Mr. Cybulski froze, a scowl etched into his face. He turned. Sofia said, "I put the rose petals in my dress." Marisia's stomach churned. She placed a hand on it. "She didn't even know. Marisia did nothing," Sofia whispered.

"You—it was you?" her father roared, drowning Sofia out. His back was broad, the shoulders hunched. "How dare you?"

Sofia clutched the skirt of her dress with her right hand, as if hanging onto a lifeline. "I don't want to marry Mr. Finley."

"What do you know? You're a sixteen-year-old girl, a mere girl with no experience of life. He has connections. He has a spotless reputation. You know nothing. Nothing! If you were a boy, I'd beat you until you couldn't stand any longer for talking like that to me. You understand? I'd throttle you."

The expression on Sofia's face was like the expression soldiers wore on parade. "In two years with Mr. Finley I'd be as good as dead. You have to understand."

Mr. Cybulski's face darkened. He lolled his head from side to side and crossed the kitchen. When he swiped the side of Sofia's head with his open palm, she tottered sideways. "I rule this household, and you'll do what I tell you." He grabbed at her hair and twisted her head close to his. "You'll go to your room! You'll not come out of that room until I say you can, not until you're ready to obey me in all things. All things! Hear that? All things!"

He flung Sofia toward the kitchen door. Shoving her ahead of him up the stairs, he followed, his footsteps crashing.

Casimir hugged Marisia's legs and swallowed his sobs, afraid to be heard. "It's all right, Casimir," she said to calm him. "He's not mad at you."

Marisia bathed Casimir's tear-stained face with a wet cloth, her own hand shaking. Should she tell Mr. Cybulski she'd thought up the plan? But what good would that do? She'd be forced from the house if he knew, and Sofia would be left completely alone.

After she'd washed his face, Marisia took Casimir into the garden. From there, she continually glanced up at Sofia's windows. Certainly Sofia was behind the fluttering curtains, but she gave no sign at all that she was there.

All the next day, the house was silent. Laying the breakfast things on the sideboard, Marisia saw Sofia's father, but he only glared once at her and turned his broad back. Quickly she exited the room, bent on staying out of his way.

In the kitchen Magdalena prepared a breakfast tray.

On it were two pieces of toast and black tea. "Is it for Sofia?" Marisia asked her.

"Yes."

"Why isn't there any jam or butter? She needs sugar for the tea."

"Orders," Magdalena snapped through thin lips. "She's to be punished, not coddled and spoiled."

"Can I take it to her?"

Magdalena held her head high on her scraggly neck and delivered the answer in a menacing voice. "Sofia insists you had nothing to do with this, but I can't believe that. She's being punished because of you."

Marisia didn't dare disagree, thinking that Magdalena for once was right. She rubbed with all her might at the ladle she was polishing. In it she could see a tiny, distorted reflection of her own face.

"You're not to communicate with Sofia. You've done enough."

The day passed slowly.

Because he seemed so listless, Marisia kept Casimir by her. He patted biscuit dough into round shapes at her direction and carried scraps to Washington. While she waxed the dining room table, Marisia told him a story that she'd once made up for Katrina about a mouse who learned to talk.

In the afternoon Marisia had her Sunday half-day off. She waited for Stefan on the porch steps in the late September heat. Overhead the sun slid from tree to tree. Still Stefan did not come. At last, as the light of the day blurred, Marisia gave up and went inside.

In her room she kept the window open in the hope that Washington would climb to her roof along the gutter spout. But even Washington had deserted her.

She took out the packet of letters from Hamburg she kept with her things, untied the string, and read through them, all nine of them in a row. In one letter Katrina was better; in another, worse. In one letter Mama sent a ticket, torn in half, from a show they'd all seen in a theater; in another, a dried, pressed fern from a woods outside the city. In one letter Papa told her to obey Magdalena; in another, he said that with any luck at all Magdalena would work herself to death before the week was out so that Marisia could rule the roost.

Marisia tied the letters up again and sat at the edge of her bed. She fingered the locket Sofia had given her on the boat. After a minute she bent and pulled out paper and Grandfather's pens from under the bed. She drew a maiden locked in a tower, who had Sofia's fine boned shoulders and graceful arms. Next she drew a dreadful dragon, which had bushy eyebrows like Mr. Cybulski's and his same thundering expression.

There was a rustle on the stairs and a knock on the door. "Magdalena told me to come," Casimir piped. "There's a man at the door."

Glad Stefan had come at last, Marisia flew down the stairs. But it wasn't Stefan who stood in the hallway. Turning his bowler hat nervously in his hands, Mr. Pulaski bowed to her. "Your brother, Marisia. It's Stefan. There's been an accident. You have to come."

"What kind of accident?"

"A box slipped from the crane at the shipping yard. Late yesterday afternoon. It smashed Stefan up. I was with him all last night. He'll live, all right, but he'll need regular nursing. They've set the bones at the hospital. They're going to release him in the morning. A nurse will be bringing him home. He won't be out of his bed for weeks they said—maybe longer than that."

"I'll come! Wait one minute. I'll pack my things!"

"Perhaps it's best that you're leaving. Mr. Cybulski isn't himself these days, not at all. I've never seen him as furious as this. Why did Sofia disobey? I've taught her to never, never disobey him. Never." Mrs. Cybulski held her hand over her forehead. "It won't go away, this headache of mine. I get them more and more often now, and nothing will make them go away, not all the powders the doctor gives me."

"Will you tell Sofia I'm gone?"

"Yes, yes, as soon as my husband allows me to speak with Sofia, I'll tell her."

"You won't forget, please."

"No, my dear, I won't forget." Mrs. Cybulski let her hand drop to her side. Her puffy lids were blue, like swollen bruises.

"She can't think I'm just forgetting all about her. Tell her I'll come back as soon as I can," Marisia pleaded. She hurried from the room.

Magdalena stood at the bottom of the front stairs. Her stringy hair was pulled back so tightly from her face Marisia couldn't understand why it didn't come right off.

"He's at the servant's entrance in the back where he belongs. He shouldn't come to the front door. The front door is for company only."

"Mr. Pulaski is just as good as anyone who ever comes to your front door," Marisia retorted. "You don't let a rule be broken ever, do you? Not ever, no matter what. What does that get you? Everyone hates you for it!"

Magdalena's tiny mouth opened in shock, then clamped tightly shut. "I do my duty," she chirped.

Marisia ran straight past her to join Mr. Pulaski at the back door. She thought no more of Magdalena. Only troubling thoughts of Stefan filled her head.

CHAPTER EIGHT

In his sleep, Stefan drew back his lips, showing his teeth and almost snarling. He reminded Marisia of an animal caught in a trap. When he woke, his eyes were blank, and he gave no sign that he recognized her or his room. Marisia helped him sip the dark tea made with herbs that Mr. Pulaski claimed would soothe his pain. She wiped his chin with a rag when the tea spilled out of his trembling mouth.

All that day, sitting by him on a wooden chair in the stifling September heat, Marisia pressed cool cloths to Stefan's face. In those long hours her thoughts trailed off to other things. What were Mama, Papa, Adam, and Katrina doing right now? Across the ocean, Marisia reminded herself, it must be night instead of day. They slept when she was awake. When she was awake, they slept. Their world was so very, very distant that it was just the reverse of her own.

The thought made her lonely, so she put it aside and

wiped the sweat from Stefan's neck. His mouth twitched, and he turned away from her. Was she doing all she should for him, all that Mama and Papa would do if they were here? Mama, she remembered, would press small, hot cupping glasses against the chest and back to break a fever. They'd make a popping sound when Mama removed them. She had none of these.

Once Stefan vomited. Marisia washed him with a damp towel, put a clean sheet on the bed, and brought him a fresh shirt. Toward evening she applied disinfectant to the open wounds on his chest, the way the nurse had shown her when she'd delivered Stefan home. Marisia adjusted the dressing on his head and put fresh bandages around his knee.

Night came. Though she struggled to stay awake, Marisia slumped down in the chair. Her head wobbled from side to side against its hard back. She slept until Stefan screamed. It was a long, high, terrifying scream that ripped Marisia's dream straight from her. She leapt from her chair and leaned over him. His eyes were closed, the lids shivering. He started to scream again, and she put her hand on his lips. "Stefan!"

He would not wake.

"Stefan, it's only a nightmare."

"No," Stefan shouted and jerked to one side of the bed as if to escape someone's hold.

The edge of the room rustled with sound. Ghosts were darting about, Marisia knew, ghosts that hoped to catch Stefan up, make him one of their own, and carry him away to the world of the dead. She stood straight up to fend them off. She stared into the room's dark corners. On the bed table, the flame of the candle wavered and sputtered because a ghost blew at it, wanting to extinguish all light. Marisia cupped the flame with her hands until it steadied.

She waited another instant, hands about the flame, almost out of breath, as if she'd been running fast. She made herself draw a slow breath in. She closed her eyes. It was then she remembered the special candles that Mama had given her the day they parted, candles that had been blessed by the priest last Candlemas Day in Lutrek. She had four of them. She dropped her hands and strode to the opposite wall. As quickly as she could, she rummaged among her things until she found them. Back at Stefan's bedside she lit one, tipping its wick into the flame of the first candle.

Candles blessed on Candlemas Day were put aside for use in storms or in sickness, Marisia knew. They were to be used in rooms, she also knew, where the dead were laid out. She leaned over Stefan, the candle in her hand. Flame flickered across his dark face. "You have to live," she whispered.

For hours she kept careful guard by Stefan, watching, praying to the Virgin, keeping the ghosts at a distance. Only when dawn came did she drop back in the chair and sleep.

In the afternoon of the second day, when she woke from another dozing slumber, Stefan mumbled, "How can you sleep sitting up like that?" His words were slurred. His reddish hair was splayed out in wild tufts above the bandages, and his face was covered with the stubble of a beard, but Stefan's eyes were no longer vacant.

"You've come back!" Marisia called to him. She clapped her hands and tossed her head, her tangled hair flying back.

"What do you mean, I've come back? From where?"

Stefan had stepped over a line, Marisia knew. On the other side of the line was death. On this side was life. The ghosts couldn't cross the line and follow Stefan here. The ghosts would not take him now. Marisia knew this for a certainty, but she couldn't say it to him. "You were in the hospital," she said instead. "You've been unconscious for days."

An hour later, Stefan took the spoon from Marisia's hand when she brought him broth and started to feed him. "I can feed myself," he insisted, but the effort to eat exhausted him. As soon as he was done, he fell asleep.

When he awoke again, less than an hour later, Stefan heaved himself to a sitting position. "What exactly is wrong with me? Why do I ache everywhere? I remember the accident, but nothing after that."

"You took a blow to the head. They said that was enough to kill most men. And your right leg is broken in two places. In the hospital a doctor set it. A rib's broken, too." Marisia stuck a pillow behind his back. "Your front tooth is chipped, and the funny thing is, it's in exactly the same spot as Papa's chipped tooth, just like his."

Stefan ran his finger over the damaged tooth. "Papa got his at about my age in a fight. I remember him telling me that."

"You sleep and sleep and sleep. Then you wake up looking so groggy anybody would think you haven't slept for days."

"Water," was all Stefan said in reply. He drank it and fell back on the pillow.

That week he slept twenty hours out of each twenty-four. Marisia kept watch over him but gradually left him more often. She cooked, shopped, and cleaned the apartment. She did laundry in a tub in the backyard, where she met a scrawny Polish girl who tilted her face back and forth when she talked and who hopped from one foot to the other like a bird.

The girl told Marisia that she longed to go to school at the settlement house, but her parents wouldn't let her. Her parents said school was for boys and that they couldn't allow her to go there unchaperoned and be thought of as a forward, cheap thing. "They act like they still live in Poland." The birdlike girl tossed her head haughtily. "They are so old-fashioned I can't stand it."

Marisia remembered how much Mama had feared her coming to America. "Maybe they're afraid for you because they care about you," she answered, missing Mama's worrying frown and her endless questions—frowns and questions she'd never thought she'd miss in all her life.

The girl only gave her a cross look and slapped irritably at the man's shirt she was scrubbing on the washboard. In the cold water the knuckles on her thin hands were an angry red. "I want to go to school, but they keep saying I'll marry a Polish boy and raise Polish children and I don't need to learn English."

"They don't want you speaking a language they can't speak," Marisia explained.

"They can learn English, then."

This girl was going to devour American foods—the Shredded Wheat cereal that Sofia's uncle sometimes ate for breakfast or the Jell-O that Marisia had seen advertised on billboards. This girl would go places her parents wouldn't, like the Coney Island she kept talking about. Before too long, like a bird, this girl would fly straight out of her parents' reach. "Maybe they're too afraid to learn English. Have you thought about that?"

The girl, like an old woman, harrumphed.

"Well, I can teach you some English words," Marisia offered. "Right now."

Nearby, a Jewish woman plucked dry laundry off the clothesline. Overhearing the lesson, she winked at a toddler who clung onto her skirt for all he was worth, listing dangerously to the left. "Listen to these girls!" she announced to him as if he'd understand. "What fine ladies they are, these girls talking their English!"

"We'll be ladies before you," the girl snapped.

"Hush," Marisia told the girl, as Mama would have told her when she was that age.

The dark-haired toddler fell over with a thump and cried out. He went on crying until his mother picked him up and plopped him on top of her laundry basket of clean clothes, where he sat like a little king on a throne. Making kissing noises at her son, her expression happy, the woman folded a pair of workman's pants and held them against her chest to smooth out all the wrinkles.

A week later, another letter arrived from Hamburg. Marisia imagined she could catch Papa's scent on the pages that she held. Papa wrote that Mama was mending and altering clothes for people while she cared for Katrina, as they'd reported in their last letter, and that he still worked at whatever odd jobs he could find. Yesterday he'd repaired someone's broken rocking chair and helped a grocer, sweeping out the store and stacking cans.

"What sort of payment can he get for jobs like that?" Stefan asked. "That means they're worse off than we are. Write back. Put two dollars in the letter. Each week now, somehow, we must send them something."

Immediately Marisia wrote to Mama and Papa and left the apartment to mail the letter. When she returned home, Stefan was sleeping. It was too hot to cook or clean, so she took out paper and Grandfather's pencils. She sat near the open kitchen window, hoping to catch a wisp of moving air while she drew.

From the alleyway two floors below came the barking of dogs. From the rooftop opposite came the sounds of someone practicing a fiddle tune and the shouts of a couple arguing. At the table, ignoring the hubbub, Marisia penciled in a castle's turrets, its drawbridge and a wall, but all the time she worked, images of Mama popped into her head.

As if following a command to do it, Marisia began a picture of Mama. First she sketched her as a queen, but in her head she could hear Mama's comment all too clearly. "Useless people, kings and queens are! What have they ever done for us?"

Marisia turned the paper around and started again.

In this sketch Mama was nothing like a queen. She carried a pail from the cowshed. Marisia caught the lift of her shoulder and her straining, muscled lower arm, the pleated wrinkling of her forehead and the twist of skin at the side of her neck. "There! That's me," she heard Mama's satisfied voice say in her head. "Now that's exactly who I am, Marisia."

Marisia turned the paper over. Her pencil darted back and forth. It felt as if someone else were working her fingers, like a puppeteer would work a puppet, someone who knew far better than she did just what she should do to make the drawing come out right.

There were Mama's rounded eyes, her slicked back hair, her blouse made of flax and embroidered in cross-stitch. Her thick fingers curled around a bowl.

At last, after more than two hours, Marisia stopped, as drained of energy as if she'd been washing floors and beating rugs for Magdalena. She touched one drawing and then another.

What had Stefan said the night before the soldiers took him, the night he had snatched away a picture she'd made of Katrina? He'd dangled it an inch from her eyes. He'd grinned crazily, the way he always did when they fought. "She looks like some fairy princess again. Why do you always draw make-believe, never-never people? Why don't you draw the Katrina who feeds pigs?"

Over and over he'd pulled the picture just out of Marisia's reach while she'd grabbed at it. "Idiot," she'd called back over her shoulder when she finally stomped away from him. "You can't draw a straight line. Who are you to tell me what's good or not? All that you're good for is shoveling out pig manure." Next she'd shouted the words she longed to take back when the soldiers marched Stefan away the next morning. "I hate you. I'll always hate you! I wish you were dead."

If he saw them, Stefan would say he'd told her to draw pictures like these of Mama months and months and months ago. Marisia hid them so Stefan wouldn't discover them and brag about how he'd been right.

The next day Marisia drew a woman bent double over her metal washboards. She drew a mangy dog curled in the sparse shade of a withered bush. She drew the fierce, birdlike Polish girl, who sat cross-legged in the dust, silver jacks cupped in her hand. While he slept, she drew a picture of Stefan on his narrow bed in the narrow room, his head bandaged, his mouth half-open, his beard half-grown, a line of sweat on the side of his face. She drew for hours that day and the next and the next.

On the first day of October, Marisia gave the month's rent money to Mr. Pulaski, who would give it to the landlord. When she spilled the remaining coins and bills from the money can onto the kitchen table, there were nine single dollars, the paper frayed with use. There was a dollar forty-two cents in pennies, nickels, dimes, and quarters. They should keep this small hoard for an emergency, Marisia thought, and not spend any more of it. That's what Mama and Papa would say.

As soon as she could leave Stefan, she must find work and make something toward their keep.

Another week passed. Stefan could rise from the bed on his own. He could cook eggs in a pan on the stove. He could hobble down the corridor to the bathroom. He could shave himself. It was time, Marisia decided.

The next day she made her way through crowded streets to the olive-packing plant by Mulberry Park, where Stefan had worked during his first weeks in New York. The man in charge wore a gray cap pulled down so far that it was hard to see his eyes. "Yes, yes, I remember him, that Stefan. Good worker, that one. Okay, yes. One lady sick. You work."

The room where he led Marisia reeked of vinegar and brine. There a half-dozen people transferred olives from great barrels into pint bottles that would be sold in shops. Gesturing, trying to talk with his hands, the man with the cap showed Marisia what he wanted her to do and pointed to a rickety chair, where she settled herself.

At lunch, in back of the building, Marisia ate the roll she'd brought and a hard piece of cheese. Leaning against the rough brick wall, her long legs sticking out in front of her, she took deep breaths of air to chase away the smell of olives. She drank water from a pump in the yard and splashed it on her face. In fifteen minutes she was called back.

That afternoon, the room grew hotter and hotter. The skin on Marisia's fingers shriveled from contact with the liquid she poured over the olives. Her neck grew stiff. She swallowed twice to fight down the sick feeling in her stomach. When the room angled sideways, she closed her eyes and fought to make it come straight up again. At the end of the day, the man who had hired her gave her a dollar and one quarter for her thirteen hours of labor. "Tomorrow, one more time, come, come!"

For three days Marisia packed olives, but on the fourth day the man with the cap shook his head at her. "Today, no. The lady not sick today, no."

At a nearby pharmacy, Marisia asked for work but was turned away. She wandered along Mott and Mulberry and Canal streets. A woman selling from a pushcart waved a silver fish by its tail to show it off and then slapped it back down on the crushed, dripping ice. Marisia stopped to watch an organ grinder, whose monkey grabbed a penny a small girl held out.

At a restaurant she tried to speak English to a woman in an apron who suddenly shook her finger in Marisia's face, screaming. "You immigrants, a bunch of no-goods, all of you! If I hire anyone to work, it's not going to be some filthy Russki or Polack or some Jew. Go on, now. Out of here. Out!" Marisia backed away from her.

At a bakery she washed dishes all afternoon. Yes, she could come back on Monday, the man who'd put her to work said to her while he looked her up and down as if he owned her. When she put her hand out for the two quarters he held up, the man grabbed the hand and jerked Marisia toward him. He put his mouth on her cheek. His beard prickled her skin. She pulled her head away.

"Let me go!"

"Just you keep quiet and nobody'll find out," he hissed.

"Stop it, stop!" Marisia said loudly.

"No noise out of you." He kissed at her neck, his arm circling her waist. He pulled her against his chest. She felt his fingers tear at the buttons on her dress.

"Don't! Stop!" She yelled the words.

He clamped one hand down on her mouth. "No noise out of you. Now isn't that what I said? There'll be no more yelling out of you."

Marisia bit at the hand on her mouth, caught flesh, and clamped her teeth tight. The hand flew back. Swearing, the man shoved Marisia hard against a wooden counter. A hand to her forehead, deliberately, he smashed her head against the cabinet behind her.

The pain shot through her. The man's face, only inches from her own, was angry. His breath reeked. Now she felt his hand at her neck. Terrified, Marisia looked about her and saw, out of the corner of her eye, a canister of flour on a shelf above her head. She made a desperate grab, caught it with her fingers, and forced the canister up, higher and higher, her arm trembling at the weight. When she tipped it above him, white flour flew everywhere. Marisia choked on it. The man did, too. It covered his hair and face, her hair and face. With a grunt, the man let her go. Slapping at his hair and beard and chest, emitting white puffs like a dragon's puffs of smoke, he spat out a string of cuss words. Outside Marisia sprinted along the cobblestoned sidewalk. Her flapping sleeves trailed flour behind her. A shoeshine boy with his kit strapped around his neck whirled to stare at her. A tan and black mongrel shot out of an alleyway and snapped at her skirt. Marisia clenched her fist and shouted at the dog until he backed away.

She marched on through dim patches of light cast by gas lamps, past men who pushed their way through the swinging doors of a saloon, past a toothless beggar who wheedled for money, past a man selling hot potatoes from a cart, past a tired-looking black man who lugged a box filled with old clothes and a pretty dark-skinned girl who clung to the edge of his coat.

Inside the apartment, Stefan was sleeping and Mr. Pulaski was nowhere to be seen. There were dirty dishes in the sink, evidence of their dinner. Marisia left the dishes where they were, lit a candle, and went to the bedroom where she folded a quilt and set it beside Stefan's bed. By the light of the candle Marisia looked at his gaunt face. Stefan opened his eyes. Drowsily, he said, "I'm sleeping," then flopped over to face the wall.

Marisia lay down on the folded quilt and pulled another over her. When she stretched out her arms, her right hand touched the frame of Stefan's bed; her left hand, the far wall. Elsa and her streets of gold—there were no streets of gold in America. There were only cramped rooms like this one with its low ceiling. The room was no bigger than a raft floating on top of an endless ocean. She clenched her teeth to keep back a cry. There was a thud on the other side of the thin wall, and another, as if people were battering their way through.

Marisia's hand twitched. Never could she tell Stefan what had happened to her, never! And Mama wasn't here to hold her and tell her what to do. She pushed herself up, throwing the quilt off. The floor was cold on her bare feet, the boards splintery.

In the kitchen Marisia took out the washbasin and filled it with water. She splashed her face and neck and rubbed the skin with a brown bar of sharp-smelling soap. A half-dozen times she cleansed herself like this before tipping the murky water into the sink. With an angry gurgling it disappeared down the drain. Marisia smoothed her clean skin and told herself no trace of the man remained, but when she turned, her own shadow on the wall made her jump and cry out.

Nothing in this room could hurt her, she told herself at once. She held perfectly still. She listened to the sputtering of the candle she'd lit. She looked from the table to the ceiling and then at the little window. She studied the corners of the room and saw the crate with paper and art supplies. She stared. Marisia went to it. She rummaged around until she found what she needed. On the kitchen table she set out paper.

With a sharp, dark pencil Marisia slashed at that paper until the man who had attacked her appeared. In fifteen minutes she had trapped him. There was his stained apron. There were the dirty creases in his round, baby face. His hands were like an animal's paws.

For a moment Marisia stared down at the man. Then, slowly, deliberately, she tore the figure into bits. She mashed the bits together in her hands and tossed them into a pan. Taking the pan to the sink, Marisia lit the paper fragments with a match. A flame leapt up. The paper blackened, crumpled into embers, and died. Marisia opened the window. Below, someone shouted up to another apartment. She shook out the ash, which caught in the wind and spun away in all directions. Her attacker was gone.

"Stefan shouldn't have had this accident," Mr. Pulaski said to Marisia. "They don't check the equipment. Four men were killed in those yards last year. The bosses don't fix what's broken, and then men go and get themselves hurt."

He tapped with one finger at the newspaper that was spread out on the table. "In here they tell about a fire in Chicago. A factory fire, I'm talkin' about. The bosses always locked the doors. Didn't want anybody slipping away from their work for a breath of fresh air. No, they never want that. So what goes and happens? Those doors are locked and that fire gets going good. Dozens dead! Men, women, half a dozen children. Ach! What a business!"

Marisia put a pinch of salt into the soup and tasted it again. She said, "It's as bad as Russia."

When he answered her, Stefan leaned forward as if facing into a stiff wind, like Papa used to do. More and more Stefan looked like Papa. Like Papa he tugged on the mustache he'd grown. Then he said, "Maybe it's like Russia, Marisia, except the president, Mr. Roosevelt, he pays attention when things go wrong. This Chicago fire

Mr. Pulaski's talking about, Mr. Roosevelt's reading about it too, don't forget. He knows, for one thing, that a lot of those workers can vote. If Mr. Roosevelt wants to be president the next time the Americans hold an election, he has to pay attention, see? And that means the workers have a chance when they decide they're going to fight back."

Mr. Pulaski picked up his paper, folded it in half, and tucked it under his arm. "Before you start talking about fighting back, Stefan, you'd better get well and get working again so you can send Marisia back to the Cybulski's house in a nice neighborhood."

Marisia stirred her soup harder. "I'm all right here." The words did not sound as certain as they would have before last night.

"These streets are no place for a young girl, not with all the riffraff you see out there." As Mr. Pulaski said this, he slipped his prized gold watch from his vest pocket. "That's my last word on the subject or I'll be late." He waved his big crooked hand at them as he left the room.

"Mr. Pulaski's right, Marisia," Stefan answered.

"Except that at the Cybulski's I'm not allowed off the front porch." Marisia stacked the plates in the cupboard, her back stiff against her brother.

"Mama would want you there." With a finger Stefan followed the groove in the middle of the table, digging out crumbs with his nail.

"I can't live in that house forever, locked away."

At those words Marisia remembered Sofia, who was

truly locked away. What was she thinking? She would have to go back.

She turned to Stefan. "What if I return to the Cybulski's house for a few months? While I'm gone, you could ask people about work for me, so I could find a real position. I don't want to be always wandering around asking for work. I hate it. But if you found something good, I'd come and live here with you and Mr. Pulaski."

Stefan laughed. "You're better off here than at the Cybulski's? Is that what you think? You liked that job packing olives, Marisia?"

"You're not my boss." Angrily Marisia slapped a lid on the soup.

When she turned around, Stefan was watching her closely. He blinked his almond eyes, ran a hand over his chin, and said, "I'm trying to do what Mama and Papa would do for you, that's all."

Stefan's crutch thudded as he moved past her. His face creased with pain. Marisia heard his sharp intake of breath. He bit his bottom lip. Watching Stefan, Marisia remembered how he'd screamed out the night after the accident and how she'd feared that if she did one thing wrong in caring for him, if she didn't do just what Mama and Papa would have done, he'd die.

"Sleep on the floor of my room forever if that's what you want," he said.

"Stefan, wait." He turned back. Marisia brushed blond strands of hair back from her face. How could she say what she wanted to say?

"When you were hurt, those first days . . . I know what you're talking about . . . about trying to take care of me the right way, the way Mama and Papa would. I'm sorry. I know you're trying to help."

Had she ever before told Stefan she was sorry about anything? She thought he'd gloat and laugh.

He didn't. Instead he tapped his crutch on the floor, underlining the words he spoke. "All right. You go back to the Cybulski's house, but only for a month or two." The look of pain eased. For a moment Stefan's face was like Papa's, as gentle as that. "I'll do what I can, Marisia. There's got to be some decent work for you around here," he said. "I'll get you something."

CHAPTER NINE

WHEN MAGDALENA TOOK THE APPLE STRUDEL from the oven, Casimir leaned close to smell it. Marisia watched her yank the dish away from Casimir's nose, her face screwed up in a frown. Magdalena didn't look like a woman who could cook anything any human could possibly swallow, but every day she turned out delicacies like this.

Marisia tucked straying hair under her white maid's cap and straightened her apron. She stepped in front of Magdalena, eyes lowered. As she'd done for the last five days, she asked, "Can I bring Sofia her tray tonight?"

Magdalena's scrawny body tightened. It looked as hard as a knot. Her voice was as hard as a knot too. "Ask me that, miss, after you've washed up all the dishes. What a lot of pots tonight!"

Casimir scrubbed the dirt from his bony knees. "I wish Sofia weren't up in that room anymore," he protested in a high voice. "I thought they'd let her out a long time ago. When I'm bad, they let me out the next day!" He stuck the tip of his tongue into the gap where his two front teeth had fallen out during Marisia's absence from the household.

When the dishes were done, Marisia asked again for Sofia's tray, eyes again cast down in a show of obedience, voice lowered modestly. There was a pause. Then Magdalena thrust a key into Marisia's hand and grumbled out orders. "That's the key to her room. Take the tray, but you're not to speak with her."

"I won't," Marisia lied. The smallest smile fluttered on Magdalena's lips. Marisia stared in astonishment at that smile — it was the smile an accomplice to a crime would wear, the only smile Marisia had ever seen on Magdalena's face in all her months spent in this house.

At once Magdalena's thin mouth shrunk back into its usual rigid line. "There is always too much to do," she complained. "They can't expect me to do it all. I don't have the time for these trays."

Hurriedly, before Magdalena could change her mind, Marisia mounted the narrow back staircase to the second floor. She turned the key in Sofia's door. Inside, a gas lamp cast a sultry light across the floor. Sofia leapt forward. Marisia's tray tipped to one side, the milk spilling. Arms circled Marisia's neck.

"Thank God!"

"Shhhh..." Marisia warned. "If they hear us talking, Magdalena won't let me come again. Did they tell you where I was?"

"No."

"Your mother didn't tell you about Stefan?"

"Father won't let her come."

"But...oh, Sofia, I didn't just desert you." Marisia set down the tray and told the story.

Sofia said, "You're here now, anyway. You don't know how glad I am you're here."

"Your father doesn't want me near you," Marisia answered.

Against Sofia's pallid skin, her eyes seemed brighter than ever, almost feverish. She leaned forward. "Father put me in here to break my spirit. He won't even give me a book to read. Not a book, not a piece of paper, not a pen. So all day long the only thing I can do is think. What do you suppose I think? That he's wrong. I can't let him give me to some, to some...to sell me off to the highest bidder." Sofia's voice trailed off.

She circled the small room twice, her steps agitated. Again she came to a stop in front of Marisia. "If he cared, he wouldn't do this to me," Sofia said. "He doesn't care, not about me, not about Mother or Casimir. Casimir has nightmares about him. All his life he's had nightmares." Out the window, the elm tree swayed in a gust of wind and its leaves rattled, a dozen of them whirling off to the ground. The same cold wind rattled the window inside its casement. It was like an alarm.

Marisia reached out and put her arms around Sofia. "If I stay longer, Magdalena won't give me the tray again."

"I won't give in, no matter how long Father keeps me here." Sofia's voice bristled in Marisia's ear. "I never thought I'd say that, but all this time alone, with nothing to do but think . . . I can see myself clearly now, Marisia, the way you can see a picture after you put a puzzle together from pieces that have been tossed into a box. I never saw it before, who I really am. I always let Father tell me what I should wear and what I should say and what I must learn." She pushed Marisia away from her. "Go on," she said. "Come back if they let you."

Magdalena scrubbed the stovetop with a wire brush. "There's one piece of strudel left," she said. "It's in the bread box on a plate. Eat it." The words were an order. In kindness Magdalena had put a piece of the dessert aside, but she didn't want the kindness to show. Magdalena had locked herself away from everyone, Marisia told herself, until she was more alone than Sofia was.

Standing at the counter, Marisia ate the strudel. Then she washed her plate, left the kitchen, and climbed the back stairs to her room on the third floor. There she lit the candle on the small dresser. She poured water from the pitcher into a washbasin. As she rubbed at her face with a wet washcloth, she heard a noise. It was Washington, who perched on the sill outside her room. He stared at her with his yellow, unblinking eyes.

When she opened the window, Washington entered. She ran her hand along his tawny fur. While she was gone, he hadn't lost weight because Casimir fed him table scraps. Surprisingly, Sofia's mother had fed Washington, too, Casimir said. He'd told Marisia that with a perplexed frown on his small face.

If anyone found her giving milk to this animal, they'd think her quite out of her mind. That's what Mrs. Cybulski had said to him. Anyone knew that if you fed strays like this, they never went away.

When Casimir asked his mother why she fed Washington if it was such a bad thing to do, she'd told him something he didn't understand. "I'm feeding him because I can. You know I can do nothing for your sister."

In the middle of the night, Marisia woke. Someone shouted. The noise came from far off. It was no concern of hers, she told herself, and pulled the covers over her head. Through the thin blankets Washington's kneading claws pricked her arm. Sleepily she pushed him away. Hitting the floor, his paws made a thudding sound. Three times he meowed. She pulled the covers down. The room was so dark she couldn't see the pest of a cat. It was then she smelled smoke.

Marisia threw the door to her room open and stepped into the hallway. Here the smell of smoke was stronger. Barefoot, she ran down the back stairs, a hand against the wall to guide her in the dark.

On the second floor, smoke poured out of a bedroom, the one in which Sofia's aunt and uncle slept each night. Through the door Marisia saw Sofia's uncle swat at small flames with a black jacket. Burning embers, like bright fireflies, swarmed around his head. Beside him, holding a bucket of water, stood Mr. Cybulski. He turned. "Don't stand there like an idiot," he screamed, his face contorted. "Do something!"

Running, Marisia grabbed a bucket of water from Mrs. Cybulski, who had dragged it from the bathroom. In the bedroom, above the place where Marisia tossed the water, flames crossed along the curtain rod. The wooden rod ignited, flaring wildly.

By Marisia's side, Mrs. Cybulski shouted to her husband, "We have to get Sofia out!"

"Get the key, then," he growled back.

"Where is it? Where? Tell me! You'd never tell me!"

"Magdalena's not to let it out of her reach! Ask her!"

Mrs. Cybulski tugged at Marisia's arm. "The kitchen. I saw her in the kitchen. Hurry." Together they ran down the corridor to the back stairs and then down the stairs themselves.

Casimir stood by the kitchen table, wiping sleep from his eyes. Mrs. Cybulski bent over him. "Go outside, Casimir. Shut the door behind you. Don't come back in. Don't dare come back in."

"I'm scared."

"Go to the neighbors, Casimir. Be quick. Tell them the house is on fire. Run now!"

As soon as the door slammed behind Casimir, Mrs. Cybulski lifted her nightdress with both hands and rushed from the kitchen, calling for Magdalena. At the bottom of the curling staircase, they found her. Magdalena watched the fire with both hands in front of her face, like a child peeking out at a monster.

"The key to Sofia's room! Give it to me!" In response, Magdalena only slumped back against the wall, then slid down it until she was sitting on the floor.

Marisia hoisted her up and stuck her hand into Magdalena's pockets. "The key, it's not in your pockets. Magdalena! Where is it?"

The answer was faint. "In the pantry... in back of the sugar canister... on a hook."

"Go outside." Marisia pushed Magdalena through the door. The rush of night air was cold. From far away, too far away, the bells of the fire trucks were ringing.

In the kitchen, Mrs. Cybulski held up the silver key. They started up the back staircase. Marisia saw that flames inched along a strip of molding in the corridor wall above them. Quickly she backed down the steps, yanked a white tablecloth from the kitchen table, held it under running water at the sink, and ran up the stairs again, taking them two at a time, the wet

tablecloth wrapped around her like a cape.

Caught in lunging smoke, one arm over her face, Mrs. Cybulski braced herself against the wall in the hall. She looked as if she'd topple over. "Let me have the key," Marisia said, wrenching it from Mrs. Cybulski's hand. "Go back down. I'll get Sofia out. I promise."

Gagging, Mrs. Cybulski retreated. Along the wall a

thread of fire seemed to follow her. In the gloom at the end of the corridor, she turned into a shadow.

From inside Sofia's room there was furious pounding. Marisia slid the key into the lock. It wouldn't turn. The hallway was as hot as an oven. Willing herself to turn the key slowly and carefully, Marisia tried again. This time the door gave. Sofia stood just inside. She waved at the smoke, her hands flying back and forth in front of her face.

The rush of air from the open door fanned the flames behind Marisia. There was a sound like an explosion and instantly the corridor turned into a tunnel of fire. From the front of the house, on the other end of the fiery tunnel, Marisia heard Mr. Cybulski call for Sofia. He called her name a second time, wailing. It was an inhuman sound, an animal's pained howl. Marisia wanted to answer. She gulped for air and coughed. She couldn't answer. She tossed the wet tablecloth around Sofia and pulled her into the corridor. Like a pair of ghosts the two girls ran.

A burning board broke from the ceiling. Sofia dodged sideways, tangling her feet in the wet tablecloth, tripping. With her bare foot Marisia kicked the board aside, biting her lips to keep from yelping at the pain. Tugging at Sofia, Marisia stumbled forward.

At the bottom of the back steps, Sofia's mother held out her arms as if welcoming Sofia and Marisia back from a long journey. In a moment they would be safe, Marisia thought, in one moment. Behind them, showering pieces of fiery wood in all directions, the ceiling collapsed. Marisia took another breath of smoking air that scorched her lungs. The awful breath, like a blow from a fist, tipped her sideways. She put her hand on the banister. For some reason Mrs. Cybulski's face and upturned arms turned black. Marisia listened to the pounding noise in her own ears and, in the moment before she pitched down the long staircase, wondered where the noise was coming from.

In the trees Marisia saw a moon. It hung like an ornament on a tall branch that swung in the wind. She moved her arm and touched leaves. Why was she lying outside on the ground? Who was the man who bent over her? She tried to focus on his face. His blond beard made a sharp point of his chin.

Nearby a woman crouched. She was asking the man something. The words were Polish and he answered in Polish. "Her pulse is normalizing now. She'll be all right. See to the others." Though the man was close, his voice seemed distant.

The woman rose as the man threw a blanket over Marisia. When Marisia tried to speak to him, the words wouldn't come. When she tried to lift her head, it fell back. It was as if her body were someone else's and wouldn't obey the commands she gave it.

"Don't try to talk," the man said to Marisia, leaning close. "You're safe. I'm a doctor. I'll take care of you. Everyone's safe." He was answering the questions Marisia couldn't seem to utter. "They all got out. Your young friend was burned slightly, but she's not in any danger. Don't worry about anything. Neighbors will care for you tonight. We'll move you in a moment."

Time and again the man brushed his hand through her scraggly hair, patiently undoing the tangles in it. Mama used to do this Marisia remembered. He seemed to be fixing everything that was wrong. "Don't worry now," he said again. She closed her eyes.

"You've slept straight through breakfast," announced a maid, a young girl with a handful of small freckles tossed across her face like flecks of sand. "I've brought you lunch. They said it must be cold liquids, so it's a chilled beef broth."

"Thank you." To Marisia's surprise, her own words were no more than a whisper.

"Dr. Heinrich is here again. That's why they wanted me to wake you."

"It's so strange. It feels as if the bed covers weigh pounds and pounds." Marisia croaked these words out. She caught the edge of the sheet in two fingers, lifted it an inch, and then let it drop.

When Dr. Heinrich came, he sat on a small upholstered chair by her bed. He was a young man and slender. For some reason—Marisia could not quite say why—he reminded her of an elf. He had long hazel eyes, magnified behind the thick glasses he wore. "We'll have you up soon," he said with a smile. "Did they tell you we sent word to your brother? We've told him that in five or six days we'll have you on your feet and send you to him. It's all arranged. They wouldn't let him off work today, but he'll come tomorrow."

Dr. Heinrich took Marisia's pulse and listened to her

lungs. He thumped her back and gave her tablets to ease the pain in her throat. When he changed the dressings on her hand and on her foot, she clenched her eyes shut so she wouldn't cry.

"I'm sorry," he said, watching her face.

As he'd done last night, Dr. Heinrich brushed Marisia's hair back. "I could speak to you in Polish. I know the language well enough, but we'll keep trying out our English here. They tell me you are trying to learn it, so we must have English conversations then. It's the only way." Marisia nodded. "You were brave to take Miss Cybulski out, you know. No, don't deny it. It's no joke to face a fire like you did. I was called to a fire once a few years ago in the tenements. I felt like a monster was coming at me."

He repeated the word *monster* in Polish for Marisia so she'd understand. "Now, wasn't it like that?" he asked. At the question Marisia remembered the burning corridor, the clawlike flames reaching for her, the pitching smoke, and the jagged noises the fire made as it rushed along the walls.

As he spooned a bitter medicine into her mouth, Dr. Heinrich imitated the face she made. "Awful stuff," he said. His small pointed beard gave him an elfish look. So did the gold-rimmed glasses and his long, narrow eyes with the web of fine lines at their corners.

"Where will the Cybulskis go?" Marisia asked him.

"Don't you worry about them. You landed here, with the Hass family. Other neighbors are taking care of the Cybulskis. Now," he added, "you're not to talk much, not with a throat looking like yours does. Rest."

For the first time, as she leaned back on the pillow, Marisia stared around her. Undoubtedly this room belonged to a girl. Lacy curtains hung at the windows, and in the corner was a delicate rose-colored chair.

"Oh, it's their daughter's room, Amanda's," the maid told Marisia after the doctor left. "They've sent her off to college this year. Can you imagine? In this household they think women should be educated to make them into doctors or teachers or I don't know what. To make them into men, my mum says. She'll never be a proper woman now, Miss Amanda. Who'd want to marry a woman who thinks she knows more than a man with all of her schooling and fancy ideas? None of it'll do her any good at all. That's what my mum says."

Marisia strained to understand these quickly spoken words. "Say it slowly. Please. My English is not so good."

"Oh, everyone tells me I talk too fast!" The girl's curls bounced about beneath her white cap. She fluffed up the quilt and settled it comfortably over Marisia. "There," she said. "You have this one last day in bed. Tomorrow we're to get you up. Your clothes are all burnt up, but the missus says she's getting you things to wear from the people at the church. So that's all right, then. Tomorrow you're to have a visitor, and we'll fix you up in a green dress of Amanda's that's ever so pretty. Especially with your coloring. I can take a tuck or two in that dress so it'll fit you. Amanda's not like you with your pretty figure."

"A visitor? Stefan? My brother?"

"No, it's a Mr. Cybulski who's coming."

"Oh."

"You should see your face," the girl said. "You don't like him much, do you?"

Marisia didn't answer out loud but shook her head no. He'd locked Sofia up, and in that prison of his, Sofia had come close to dying. What could she possibly say to Mr. Cybulski?

"Well, like it or not, you'll have to see him," the girl declared. "There's what you like and the practical facts of the matter, my mum always tells me. Expect she's right, too."

CHAPTER TEN

MR. CYBULSKI'S STEADY GAZE dropped to Marisia's bandaged hand. "That's all? The one hand?"

"That and my foot," Marisia replied.

"Yes, the bandage there, I see it," Mr. Cybulski said. He nodded at the sofa "Be seated." He turned his back on her as he uttered that command. When he moved in front of the fireplace, the flames leaned toward him.

Marisia stood in place, her eyes watching Mr. Cybulski's back, which was as solid as a wall. She heard him say, "It's bitter cold outside. It's as cold as it ever was in Poland." She waited through a minute of silence until Mr. Cybulski spoke again. "They told me you took in a great deal of smoke, that you're lucky to have gotten out alive. If you hadn't, I'd have that on my conscience, too."

Rubbing his hands together, he turned toward her. Abruptly he asked, "Does it hurt your throat to speak?" Quickly, before she could answer his question, he did. "It must."

He looked past Marisia, as if at someone else, although the room was empty except for them and silent except for the noise the fire made. Outside a band-tailed pigeon settled on the hawthorn tree that still held a few clusters of red berries. The bird tilted back his head and cracked a berry so big it seemed he would choke on it. He downed it and immediately pecked at a second one. Marisia wondered why this wild pigeon was in the yard at the end of October when other birds had migrated.

Mr. Cybulski's voice crackled like the flames. "I couldn't see that you'd saved Casimir on the ship. My pride wouldn't let me see it. Now you've saved my daughter. Mrs. Cybulski insists you did so. They all say that. I must agree." Mr. Cybulski's neck was so short that his head seemed to rest directly on his rounded shoulders, like the head of a snowman. "Have they told you?" he asked.

"Told me what?"

"She's disfigured."

"What do you mean?"

"Sofia's face. She'll no longer be the great beauty. That doctor says there's nothing they can do. When the bandages are off, she'll be marked by fire all along one side of her face."

"Oh, no. No!"

In a rush the band-tailed pigeon flew up.

Mr. Cybulski said, "I can't believe it. You don't know how it was. When Sofia was twelve and thirteen, everyone said what a match she would make. I was a lucky man, they said, producing such a beauty. Her scars — they're a torment sent to punish me."

Marisia dropped her bandaged left hand into the palm of her right hand. It throbbed painfully. *"Your* torment!" she burst out, her blue eyes clouding with anger. "Do you know what *she's* suffering? Her face feels as if it's still on fire. Do you know that?"

When Mr. Cybulski scowled, Marisia waited for his thundering response, but he only stared silently again at the far side of the room. He stared so hard that Marisia turned to look in that direction. Of course, there was no one. Perhaps Mr. Cybulski had found a spirit hovering there, she thought. Perhaps he talked to it. "Sofia tells me she doesn't care that her beauty's destroyed."

A minute passed before Mr. Cybulski turned his face toward Marisia once more. "I told you to sit," he said. "Why don't you sit?"

Marisia made herself stare straight back at him. "I prefer to stand," she said. One day, she determined, she would put Mr. Cybulski into a picture for Katrina. He would be the North Wind, blowing up a great storm of clouds and hail, his cheeks puffed, deep furrows lining his forehead, his tousled, angry beard askew, his lips swollen like now.

The lips moved. "What else is there for a girl but marriage? He was fabulously wealthy, that Finley. I thanked God that Finley's mother was Polish, with plain origins, they said. It was lucky for us the father was dead because he'd never agree to a match like this, a girl with no connections to speak of. How could Sofia turn her back on a chance like this? Damnation! How could she, by all that is holy?" His voice rose to a bellow. "When I was her age...as a child, you can't imagine —" He stopped abruptly. His hands curled into fists. When Mr. Cybulski spoke again, the words were halting.

"If I ate at all in the winter time, it was cabbage and beets that we'd carry up from the cold cellar dug underneath our house. A house, I call it. One poor room with a dirt floor—that's all it was." His eyelids shut. "There were times we didn't even have cabbage and beets. Nothing at all. A sister of mine died one winter. We were so hungry, and it was so damnably cold. That spring the cold didn't break. There was ice on the ground in May on Saint Stanislaus Day. I remember it."

Hands clamped together in front of him, Mr. Cybulski paced back and forth. "I never speak of it, do you hear me? But I'll tell you, when I saw my very daughter turning her nose up at diamonds and carriages, I... what does she want?"

"Ask her," Marisia whispered fiercely.

Mr. Cybulski stopped pacing and faced Marisia. "Ask Sofia? Her head's filled with romantic notions. She hasn't any sense."

"Yes, that's why you locked her up."

"How dare you say such..." Flinching, Mr. Cybulski jerked his head sideways. "I can't stop myself. I all but killed Sofia and still I go on...."

The room was stuffy and hot, but Mr. Cybulski bent very close to the fire. It seemed to lick his outstretched hands.

Five days later, Marisia sat inside a carriage that passed through swirling snow. It settled like a veil on sloping lawns and on housetops. Beside her, Dr. Heinrich rustled his feet. Marisia saw that his shoes were scuffed from wear. "I'm too busy to give them a proper shine," he said, bracing one shoe on his knee and quickly wiping at it with the cuff of his great fur overcoat.

Marisia blushed. How had Dr. Heinrich read her thoughts?

"Don't mind your noticing," he laughed. "It shows intelligence, noticing little things like that. It's the sort of perception a doctor must have. We pay attention to details that nobody else would notice. It's how we come to discover what's wrong with a patient."

As before, Dr. Heinrich spoke slowly and mixed Polish words with his English ones so that Marisia could understand. "How do you know Polish?" she asked him.

"When I was very young," Dr. Heinrich explained, "I had a Polish nanny who took care of me. We spoke Polish, of course, the two of us. In those days I spoke Polish with my nanny, French with my French mother, and German with my father. Until I was four or five, I thought everyone talked in three languages at home."

He took his large fur hat from his head and put it in his lap, then stroked it as if it were some animal that had nested there. Light flashed along the rim of his gold glasses when he tilted his head. "Wait until you see the city in the snow. It's another place entirely. Would you like to go through Central Park on our way? There are a half a million trees there, they tell me, though I've never counted them myself, I have to confess." His eyes shone with excitement, so that he reminded Marisia for an instant of Adam or Katrina. He might, she thought, jump with excitement the way a child would, in spite of the fact that he was an adult, a man, she guessed, who was twenty-seven or twenty-eight years of age. Just as she thought this, Dr. Heinrich did jump up.

"I'll tell the driver." He leaned his head out the window and called up to the top of the carriage.

In the park the carriage followed tracks pressed into the ground by others. They circled a pond, where people skated on the  ice. Branches of trees dangled down under the weight of snow. Clumps of snow fell onto the back of a hound racing through them. He shook himself. The snow flew off in all directions.

Dr. Heinrich drew a silver watch out of his vest pocket. "We'll give ourselves fifteen minutes outside if you like. I'm afraid that's all the time I have to spare."

They strolled along the side of the road. Pulled by a chestnut horse, a sleigh passed. Cold air streamed from the horse's nostrils. Nearby, one screeching boy was burying another who lay spread-eagled on the ground.

"My brothers and I," Marisia said, "once buried my little sister in a pile of snow. When we went to dig her out again, all the piles of snow looked the same and we couldn't find her. The dogs had to sniff her out for us. She'd practically frozen by that time. I took off my coat and Stefan took off his coat and Adam too, and we wrapped her up in the whole bundle of them!"

Dr. Heinrich laughed. She said, "Stefan was worse with me."

"I can't imagine worse."

"One thing he'd do, he'd pretend he was possessed by the spirit of some dead person. He'd have a fit and shake all over. Then he'd tell me exactly how he died—some bloody, awful death of course, every single time. He'd keep this up until I was so frightened I'd cry—I was maybe four or five—and then all of a sudden he'd fall over on the ground. When I shook him, he'd wake up. He'd pretend he couldn't remember his fit or his gory stories. I'd feel sorry for him. Being possessed by spirits—it seemed so horrible that I never told on him."

Dr. Heinrich smiled. Tiny creases appeared all around his eyes when he did, like spokes off the hub of a wheel.

Marisia said, "Don't ask me what other things we've done to each other. There are so many, it would take hours to tell you." She sifted a handful of snow from one hand to the other "If Katrina were here, if Adam were here, I'd bring them to this park. This is almost like being in Lutrek—all these trees and the hills."

With a sharp pang she longed for their stream and the aspen grove behind their house that paled to a ghostly white in the winter when the trees had dropped all their leaves. In Lutrek the wind passing through that grove was a spirit's raspy breathing. It was the breath of a man who had hunted on Sunday mornings, the story went, when others were attending Mass, as everyone should. Now dead, he was made to wander in that grove for all eternity and warn others that no one must hunt there on a Sunday as he had.

That's the tale she'd heard when she was little. That's what she'd told Katrina only last year.

That afternoon Stefan showed Marisia a room that was even smaller than his own. It was hardly bigger than a closet, with just enough space for a narrow bed. He pushed his hand through his shock of reddish hair and told her, "It's not big, but you get it all to yourself. It's better than sleeping on my floor. It was part of another apartment to begin with. But when those tenants moved out, Mr. Pulaski said we'd wall it off and put a door in the wall and pay the landlord more than he'd make otherwise. When there's money to be made, landlords always go along with a plan. Anyway, you'll be living with us across the hall and just sleeping here, really."

"It's fine."

"I rounded up these crates for you. You can store your clothes in them and stash them under the bed." Between two fingers Stefan massaged his earlobe while he talked. "You'll be all right then?" When Marisia nodded, he left her by herself to unpack her things.

That night, Marisia could not fall asleep. She must sleep, she told herself, because Stefan would wake her at quarter to five in the morning. She must be at Mrs. Clay's shop on Delancey Street by six. Stefan said she'd be nice, this Mrs. Clay. He'd searched for a long while and so had Mr. Pulaski to find an employer who was said to be fair and decent. Some even said this Mrs. Clay was kind.

The bed linens and table linens that were produced in Mrs. Clay's shop were among the finest in the city, Stefan had claimed. Marisia would work as a seamstress. After a year or two in the shop, Stefan had told her, the girls who were successful in their apprenticeships were sometimes asked to embroider the beautiful designs Mrs. Clay was known for. If Marisia were successful, if she were given such an assignment, she might receive an additional fifty cents a day in her wages. There was, Stefan had said, a future in the work.

"You like to draw," he had added. "So I thought you would like embroidering designs one day. I thought it was just the right job for you."

"It's perfect," Marisia had answered. But now, lying in her bed, unable to sleep, she thought of how often she had been bored when darning socks in Lutrek or hemming skirts. She would hurry through such tasks so that she would not have to sit still any longer than was necessary.

Mrs. Clay was almost as wide as she was tall. Except for a reassuring grin that spread across her face, she was witchlike, with a pointed nose, frizzy auburn hair, and little round eyes. She led Marisia first to a table where a pot of tea and cups were set out.

"When I began, nobody gave me tea," Mrs. Clay said, as she poured a cup and handed it to Marisia. "Wasn't it the wee lass I was. Eight years old was all, and never one moment to rest. Indeed I'd cry sometimes because I was so tired. My girls, now, I let them fill their cups as often as they like from this teapot."

Done with her tea, Marisia did as Mrs. Clay bade. She rinsed the cup with water from a pitcher, tossing the rinse water into a basin, and then set her cup near the teapot again. Next, she followed Mrs. Clay to a long table where three girls were sitting. Two had dark hair. The first dark-haired girl had a narrow nose and brown eyes, and the second, a wide nose and blue eyes. The third girl, a girl with light brown hair, did not look up at all when she was introduced so Marisia could not tell what color her eyes were, but her name, Mrs. Clay said, was Rose.

Rose continued to peer at her embroidery work while Ellen gave Marisia a shy smile and said, "I am very glad to make your acquaintance."

"Welcome to our table," Hattie said. She was a big, broad-shouldered girl with eyes that laughed.

"You must turn your chair into the sunlight," Mrs. Clay said, as Marisia took a seat at the table, "or it is blind you will be before the year's out. Sure now, if God gave us sunshine, we must make good use of it."

Her words were so thick with Irish brogue that Marisia couldn't recognize half of them. When she admitted this, Mrs. Clay laughed. "In Ireland, we put music into the speech. You may depend on it. 'Tis the Americans who will take the music right out again and call that progress!"

Mrs. Clay sat beside Marisia as she explained how Marisia was to hem a linen tablecloth, using only the smallest of stitches. When Marisia began to sew, Mrs. Clay watched her for a full minute with a critical eye. "Good," she said finally. "That's fine, then. When you finish with this, come and show it to me. Today I must check every single piece of your work before I give you another." Then Mrs. Clay rose. She walked away on her short legs, bobbing up and down. On the other side of the room she sliced at great bolts of cloth with even strokes of her black scissors.

Toward the end of Marisia's second week of work at Mrs. Clay's, on a Friday, all the girls were let off at mid-day. "I must travel up to Boston," Mrs. Clay explained. "Last night a double blessing descended upon my sister's household. A baby we were expecting and then, God bless us, another came right upon the first. Twins she had and that makes seven and wore out with it all she is before she's even started. She says she needs someone by her. Certainly I'll be going. A sister need not ask a second time."

She tucked the two weeks' wages into Marisia's apron pocket. "We won't have a Friday half-day and a Saturday off again for a long, long time, saints preserve us. A lucky girl you are with a holiday and money in your pocket, both at the same time. Now then, off with you!"

Marisia traced her way through the streets. On

Broadway she stared at the grand columns and arches of a corner building that made her think of a palace, except that ordinary people passed in and out of it. No czar forbade their entering. No uniformed soldiers stopped them.

A woman who saw Marisia staring up stopped directly in front of her. "That's the Haughwout Building. There's an elevator inside that whisks one up from floor to floor. It's like riding on a magic carpet!" She said this proudly, as if the building were her very own, then walked on and disappeared into the crowd.

As Marisia traveled north through the city, the streets grew more splendid. Brightly colored carriages passed, some with footmen who rode high on top, bundled against the cold in great overcoats, heads erect. Occasionally automobiles stormed past, and the horses shied away, tossing their heads. In the window of one shop, Marisia stared at a hat made of rose  colored velvet with a crown of plaited silk. On the silk were pictured roses with curling green leaves.

How she'd dreamed that in coming to America she would turn into a fine lady and wear hats like this one! Her hand was on the doorknob. She hesitated. She could never buy anything in a shop like this, she reminded herself. But then she thought that it couldn't hurt just to try the hat on. A small bell tinkled when Marisia stepped inside.

The hat was in Marisia's hand. Sitting on a stool in front of a mirror, she placed it on her head. The girl who stared back, the girl in the rose hat, had pretty, teasing eyes. Marisia turned her neck to view herself from the side. Even her nose, its profile roughened, seemed suddenly elegant.

Behind her, Marisia heard voices. In the very right-hand corner of the mirror she saw two young ladies dressed in finery, one a black-haired girl and the other a strawberry blond. Openly they stared at her, and at once, in the mirror, Marisia saw what they did—a plain girl from the streets wearing a dress of sturdy gray cotton, its white collar worn thin. That girl wore a ridiculously fine hat on her head. Abruptly Marisia took the hat off.

The dark-haired girl called out, "That hat certainly becomes you." When Marisia said nothing, she called again, "Why don't you answer when you're spoken to?"

Marisia turned on the stool to face the girl's mocking eyes. She spoke in the perfect ladylike tones she'd so often practiced with Sofia. "I like the hat quite well. Indeed, it's exactly the hat I've been looking for."

She rose and passed to the counter. To the shop girl she said, "I'd like to purchase this hat. Wrap it for me, please." Marisia, with one quick turn of her head, saw the look of surprise on the dark-haired girl's face. In Marisia's hand was the precious roll of bills Mrs. Clay had given her. The hat would cost all but half a dollar of her two weeks' salary. Mouth dry, but eyes firm and head held high, she handed the money across the glass countertop.

CHAPTER ELEVEN

MARISIA PUT HER PACKAGE underneath the bed. She sat on the thin mattress and stared straight ahead at the wall. There, two cracks formed a V. The V, pointing to the floorboards, looked like a symbol that marked the way to buried riches on a treasure map, but if she pried the floorboards up, Marisia knew, there would be no shimmering treasure that could restore the money she had spent. This was not a storybook.

The harsh voice in her head drummed on and on. Weeks of grocery money and rent money, the voice accused, for a hat with roses on it! Where could she ever even wear such a hat? To work at Mrs. Clay's, where the girls would stare as if Marisia had gone mad? To attend services in the little Polish church? To buy lemon drops at the candy store near Hamilton Fish Park?

Marisia put her hands up to her ears to block the voice out. Drawing her knees up, she lay down sideways on the bed.

Minutes later, through a thin wall that divided her room from an outside corridor, she heard a door slam. It would be Stefan or Mr. Pulaski coming home, Marisia guessed.

She wouldn't tell Stefan what she'd done, not tonight. He didn't expect her to be paid until tomorrow. Maybe by then...what?

What miracle could possibly occur that would give her two weeks' wages in one day? Marisia made herself stand up. She brushed the folds out of her skirt and tied back her straggling hair. She crossed the hall to the apartment.

His elbows on the kitchen table, his blue work shirt unbuttoned at the top, Stefan looked at Marisia with a lifeless expression. "What is it?" Marisia asked.

"This." He fingered a letter on the table, its right side covered with German stamps.

"What?"

"Read it." Stefan held the letter out.

Marisia grabbed at it but didn't dare to open it once it was in her hands. "Tell me."

Stefan said nothing. He only rubbed at his temples with his fingers as if to ease a headache.

"Stefan..."

He dropped his hands to the table. On the ridge of the palms below the fingers were calluses. "She's coughing blood all day. She can hardly sit up."

Quickly Marisia read the few lines Papa scrawled. The unkempt letters slanted and wavered on the page, so unlike his usual steady handwriting.

Stefan cracked the knuckles on his left hand, making the popping noises Marisia hated. He seemed to want to pull himself apart. When he spoke, Stefan's voice cracked, too. "We'll send them everything we've saved. Maybe there's something they can do. We'll take all we can out of tomorrow's pay."

"Yes," Marisia agreed. Without a sound, she began to cry.

"We don't take returns, miss."

"Please. I haven't even untied it. You can see it hasn't been opened."

"It's not the package, it's a matter of store policy, miss." The girl rolled one blond ringlet of hair around a finger. On the finger was a ring with an eye-shaped green stone. Catching the light from overhead, the green eye winked at Marisia, seeming to taunt her.

"I wouldn't usually ask to return something that I..." What was the English word for *purchased*? Marisia's mind went blank and she couldn't finish the sentence.

A tall woman looking at bracelets on the counter stared at Marisia as Marisia pleaded with the salesgirl. Under that stare, Marisia felt her face flush, but she made herself go on. "I can't buy the hat. My sister is very sick. I must send money to my mother."

Busily the salesgirl straightened a row of gloves. "I'm sorry." She moved further down the counter.

"May I see it?"

Marisia turned. The tall woman's face was heavy with wrinkles. The gray curls covering her head were

rigid, as if made of metal. In her own hands was an afternoon hat with a satin brim and egret plume, which she set aside. "Open the package, and let me see this hat of yours," she commanded. Obeying, Marisia pulled at the bow. The package fell open. Her eyes pinched halfway closed, the woman held Marisia's hat at arm's length to inspect it. Her fingernails were sharp, the fingers short and bent, like talons on a bird.

"At least you show good taste. You shouldn't be buying things like this, it's true," she said in a voice as deep as a man's, "but I can see how this one tempted you."

Facing the little counter mirror, the woman perched the hat on her head. She stared at the hat itself and at the mole high on her right cheek, as big as a penny, at the large hooked nose and the bright, pursed mouth. She smiled at her own reflection and gave a satisfied nod. "Perfect! It's just what I want, my dear. I'll gladly pay you whatever you paid for it."

To the shop girl, without really looking at her, the woman said, "Wrap it again, please."

"Yes, right away, madam."

Outside the shop the woman faced Marisia. "I didn't want to ask inside, in front of that twit of a girl, but whatever possessed you to buy such a hat in the first place? How much money can you possibly make in a week? What do you do, my dear, for a living?"

As Marisia answered her questions, the woman asked more of them. Strolling with this stranger past tall brownstones with flower boxes set on their porches, Marisia talked of life in the tenement blocks. She told how she drew late at night when everyone else slept and of how it had all started when she'd made the first surprising drawings of Mama.

Startled at herself for revealing so much, Marisia asked a question of her own. "Why do you want to know all this?"

"Oh, I collect people—of all varieties, in all shapes and sizes. It amuses me to do so," the woman answered. "Other people might collect coins or stamps for amusement, I suppose. My own sister collects teacups. Coins, teacups, that would never do for me, I'm afraid. I do find people so much more interesting." Her voice was as dry as sand. She tightened her hand around the fur collar of her cape. On three of her fingers, below ridged knuckles, were diamond rings.

"You are quite an interesting child. I saw that in the shop when you faced down that girl behind the counter." The woman said this, then stopped in the middle of the sidewalk, forcing other pedestrians to walk around them. She didn't seem to notice that she was in the way. "Are we going in the right direction, my dear? I haven't been paying any mind at all. You must take me to your lodgings. I'm very interested in these dozens of drawings you say you've made."

The woman swept a hand along the side of her head to adjust her stiff curls. "But you don't even know my name. It's Mrs. Heatherston." She tapped with her pointed fingernails on the very tip of her chin. Her slanting eyes were a curious yellow brown. Marisia had the momentary sharp impression that she was prey and that this woman was swooping toward her from out of the sky. She shook the thought out of her head. She was only going to be collected like a teacup, not gobbled up like a mouse.

"Let's walk, shall we?" Mrs. Heatherston asked. "It keeps the heart strong. It fills the lungs. It's very good for you, my dear. Every day one should walk. Oh, I walk daily. Yes, I certainly do."

"I'd suffocate in here in an hour. It's unimaginably cramped," Mrs. Heatherston said as she surveyed the room. At once Marisia saw this space through this woman's eyes—the worn floorboards, the low ceiling with its chipped plaster, the faded quilt on the narrow bed whose coil of springs sagged tiredly.

"I see that you're blushing. Don't be embarrassed at my comments, my dear. I simply have the habit of speaking the truth. I've read about tenement conditions, the squalor in these streets, the disease, babies dying of dysentery, God knows what. But then none of this is your own fault, is it? You're not the one who should be blushing."

Mrs. Heatherston turned her head slowly from side to side as she talked, the way a person on a stage might when surveying a large audience. Certainly there was no audience anywhere in this room, Marisia thought. There was barely room for the two of them.

Mrs. Heatherston interrupted that thought. "But your drawings, my dear. That's why I'm here."

One by one Mrs. Heatherston held Marisia's pictures into the thin beam of light from a window that faced the airshaft. She murmured, as if talking to herself, "They are better than I expected, far better. These earlier ones don't count for much, of course. They simply indicate you can draw a bit, like other girls your age, but these later ones..." Mrs. Heatherston tapped on the drawing Marisia had made of the young woman who sold her eggs on Orchard Street. She wore her hair coiled above her head like a crown and had a proud, self-assured face. "You've captured an expression that reveals her. Yes, you make us feel we can see straight into her. You wouldn't argue with *her* about the price of eggs, would you?"

The fur cape slipped down on Mrs. Heatherston's shoulders, its gold buttons pointed at the ceiling like staring eyes. Suddenly she clasped Marisia's chin between two fingers and tilted it up. She studied it as she had studied Marisia's drawings. "As for you," she said, "you are very much alive. One can see that in your face. Very alive. You look as if you're about to burst into song."

Abruptly Mrs. Heatherston dropped her fingers and turned to the door. "I can find my own way out," she announced.

Before Marisia could say anything in return—she'd said nothing at all since they'd come into the room— Mrs. Heatherston was marching down the wooden staircase. Her heels stamped nosily on each step. Marisia heard the front door to the building bang shut.

In the following weeks, Marisia worked at Mrs. Clay's from six in the morning until six in the evening. Sometimes during those hours, Mrs. Clay read snatches of newspaper aloud, declaring every time that her girls must not be ignorant of the world and must listen closely. Marisia found out about the striking coal miners and women marching for the right to vote and the Boer wars in South Africa. She learned that Alice Roosevelt, the daughter of the president, smoked cigarettes and that there was a skyscraper in Madison Square twenty stories high and that people staying at the Waldorf Hotel kept a lion for a pet and that a man had crossed the Irish Channel in a hot-air balloon.

Each day Marisia felt more comfortable speaking English. She thought about the fiery, birdlike girl she'd met in the back yard months ago. She could teach her hundreds of words now if the girl were still about, but she and her family had vanished without a word. Marisia had no idea what had happened to them.

The needle pricked Marisia's fingers. She gave a start. She bent closer to the lace she was attaching to a pillowcase. Carefully she slid the needle through cloth. Up and down the needle went, time and time and time again.

During these weeks, Stefan sent all the money they could manage to save to Papa and Mama, but there was no word until one bitterly cold day in December. Only three days before Christmas, Marisia took a letter from their mailbox at the bottom of the stairs. It was, she knew, from Papa. She tore it open.

Papa wrote that on the eighth of December, early in the morning, just after the church bells had rung out five o'clock, Katrina had died. At the bottom of the envelope, tied with a piece of blue thread, was a curl of her hair.

The sounds in the building—the slap of shoes on stairs, a shout, a baby's wail—seemed to come from miles away. Louder than all that was the rushing sound inside Marisia's own head, like crazily flowing water. It seemed, too, that she saw the wall and the mailbox with its cracked metal flap through water. It was the way they shivered before her eyes. She held a fist against her chest and struggled for air.

Hands were pushing her down, drowning her, holding her under. The light darkened. The air churned. When she inhaled, Marisia choked. The hands pushed harder.

Twisting, Marisia lunged to the door to escape them and shoved with all her might. She ran down the steps to the street, stumbling at the bottom into a man who shouted at her when she pushed past him. Hard winds whipped her. She heard a sob—another and another. Only after a minute did Marisia realize these gagging cries were her own.

Katrina had been dead for two weeks. All this time she had led her life as if nothing at all had happened. With Stefan she had returned to Central Park. There they'd gone sliding across a frozen pond, laughing when they fell. She'd searched and searched the stalls along the streets for Christmas gifts. She'd cut out figures from cardboard—

shepherds and Joseph, the Christ Child and Mary—and placed them in a hut of twigs for a Nativity scene. She'd talked endlessly with Mr. Pulaski about how they must do things Mama had always done on Christmas Eve—spread a thin layer of hay under the tablecloth in memory of the manger where the Godchild was born, light a candle in the window to welcome Him, break the Christmas wafer, the *oplatki* that was stamped with the figures of Mary and the Christ Child and the angels. They must prepare *kutia* of nuts and raisins, honey and wheat. In these weeks she'd thought of little but celebration, and all that time Papa's letter had been coming closer and closer.

For an hour Marisia walked aimlessly. Finally, exhausted, she found her way back to Ludlow Street. In front of the building she buried her nose in the rough sleeve of her coat, her arms crossed in front of her face. When Marisia exhaled, the air turned into ghostlike puffs. She stomped her feet to warm them. From the tenement synagogue two doors down the street, through a door held open by two women, came the keening, lonesome notes of a male voice singing.

At last she could put the moment off no longer. Marisia raised her head. In apartments above, windows were filled with dull light. She mounted the splintered wooden steps.

By now Stefan would be home. She must bring him the letter.

Christmas passed. The first week of January passed. Marisia constantly felt tired, too tired to move. Each night, rather than talk with Mr. Pulaski and Stefan at the kitchen table over evening tea, rather than crochet or fix a special pudding, she went across the hall to her cold room and collapsed on her bed. One night Stefan followed Marisia there and pulled the quilt down. He asked if he could get her something and she told him she didn't want anything at all. Stefan put his face in his hands.

In those weeks, Marisia lost weight. Mr. Pulaski, his face creased with worry, told her to eat more. Marisia told him she'd turned into a bear that wanted to hibernate and sleep the winter away and not eat at all.

Of course she could not stay in a cave like a hibernating bear.

Each day Marisia went to Mrs. Clay's and did what she was told to do. There, she took no interest in what had interested her before — the news from the paper, the series of new embroidery designs, the stories Mrs. Clay told of her childhood life in Ireland, or the songs from the vaudeville shows that the girl named Hattie tried to teach them. Dutifully Marisia hemmed tablecloths or finished sheets and pillowcases. She nudged needle through cloth. She could do no more.

On the second Sunday in January, Dr. Heinrich appeared. He brought Sofia with him. Her bandages were gone, and Marisia could see the scar in the shape of a large paw burned into her face. It looked as if an enormous dog had slapped at her cheek and left a raw, gray mark streaked with red. From hairline to neck, the mark covered all of one side of Sofia's face. All around it,

Sofia's skin was crimped and puckered. In spite of herself, Marisia winced. Sofia saw and lowered her head, her smile tightening.

As they sat at the kitchen table, Sofia squeezed Marisia's hand. "Marisia, you still look so exhausted. You still have those awful circles under your eyes. You said Mrs. Clay was kind, but she had you back at work the same week you found out Katrina died."

"Maybe work is what I need," Marisia replied. "Maybe if I'm busy sewing, I won't think as much about everything else." She looked at Dr. Heinrich, who rubbed specks of dirt from his glasses with the tip of his jacket. "All those things, remember how I said we could be so mean to Katrina, Stefan, and I . . ."

"What you told me in the park about the tricks you'd play on her, burying her in the snow?" Dr. Heinrich asked. Like a boy, he hitched his feet up on the rungs of the wooden chair. He wedged the curling ends of the gold frames behind one ear and then behind the other. He pushed the glasses up on the bridge of his nose. Now, when Dr. Heinrich faced her, his hazel eyes were magnified.

"I wish I could undo every bad thing I ever did to Katrina—throwing eggs at her in the barn, all kinds of things."

Dr. Heinrich leaned his elbows on the table, his face close to Marisia's. "This is real life, you know. Perfect people who are never mean to sisters live only in stories."

"In fairy tales," Marisia said. "No, fairy tales don't really happen. I've learned that."

"Anyway, those eggs you threw at Katrina, that's not what killed her. Not that, and not covering her up with snow. Believe me." Shifting his chair sideways, he crossed his legs. He stared at the tip of his shoe while Sofia tapped her spoon on the side of her cup.

Sofia spoke. "Don't you remember when you made a dress out of newspaper for Katrina and she said you were the best sister ever? One day on the boat. Remember?"

In the kettle, the boiling water rattled. Marisia threw tea into a chipped teapot and set out cups, which did not match. Once she would have given anything to have a fine china service with matching teacups and saucers. There had been one afternoon, as a matter of fact, in the Lutrek of her childhood, when she and Elsa had designed the china set each one was sure to own one day. Marisia remembered the hours they'd spent on their mindless, intricate drawings.

A drizzling afternoon it had been with Elsa humming away as they sketched. Now, fine china or cracked cups, none of it seemed to really matter. Absentmindedly, caught up in her own thoughts, Marisia stared across the table at Sofia.

"Don't, Marisia. Don't stare at it like that," Sofia pleaded, covering the scar on her face with a hand.

"I didn't mean to, Sofia. I was just..."

"Everybody stares. Now people say, 'Oh, you know, Sofia Cybulski, the one with the burns on her face.' That's all I am to them."

Marisia saw Dr. Heinrich look at Sofia. He wore the expression he'd worn the night of the fire when he'd brushed her own hair back from her face and told her that she was safe. He opened his mouth, ready to say that to Sofia, Marisia fancied. He ran a hand over his mouth instead and closed it. He took a long breath and let it out.

"Father was so strict," Sofia said. "I was not to have a single flaw. I was supposed to be absolutely perfect. I never threw an egg at anyone. It wasn't allowed. Do you know what he would have done to me if I'd thrown an egg? Can't you see him? I wasn't allowed to be a real person. Never. Not ever. I was this...this doll that he thought was his, that had no flaws of any kind."

Sofia's voice was roughened and forceful. If she didn't see Sofia in front of her, Marisia realized, she wouldn't know that it was Sofia speaking, the Sofia who had always talked with her mouth half-closed against her own words.

"But now I can't be perfect. It's impossible, so I must learn to be real instead." Sofia brushed her hand across the blemished wood of the table. "I want to be real and accept that I'm real. Father can't. He can't accept my scars. He'll hardly look at me."

"If you must learn to be real," Dr. Heinrich said after a pause, "I can introduce you to someone who can teach you. I stop sometimes at the Henry Street Settlement House to see an old woman I operated on in the hospital. She's not perfect at all. She's got a bellowing voice. Half her teeth are gone. She's so real, she makes my teeth rattle, but she's a favorite of mine all the same."

Sofia's eyes brightened. "Well, I will ask her to give me lessons then," she said.

"She tells the wildest stories about this childhood of

hers on the frontier in the eighteen forties," Dr. Heinrich went on. "Hunting bear with her father, trapping beaver, breaking horses—she's done it all. She's wonderful, really. By her account, she's risked death dozens of times." Dr. Heinrich's long firm eyebrows turned up elfishly on the ends and his eyes laughed.

Sofia stood up and laughed back at him. "All right. Take me to her." Though Dr. Heinrich was, Marisia guessed, at least ten years older than Sofia, at that moment they seemed to her to be exactly the same age.

On the sidewalk, Marisia waved as their carriage rolled away. At the end of the block, when it rounded the corner, Marisia turned back. She sat on the stoop of her building in a patch of sun, as other people were doing up and down the block because the day was so surprisingly warm for January. Small clouds skittered across the sky. Hung out to dry on clotheslines that were strung from fire escape to fire escape, laundry surged in the wind. The sheets suspended there were as buoyant as the clouds themselves.

Suddenly, in the street a horse whinnied and reared up. When it broke away from the man who held it by a rope, its hooves clattered on the paving stones. A woman waved her shawl at the horse, trying to head it off. A fat man made a grab at it. The horse veered out of the fat man's way, jumped, and careened into a cart. Apples spilled. As they rolled in all directions, four little boys and a girl scrambled after them. The horse now leapt at the woman with the shawl. She threw the shawl right over the horse's head, while the man who'd let him loose in the first place caught the horse by the tail.

Life wasn't stopping because Katrina had died. Here was the proof right in front of her, Marisia realized. Like a horse that had broken free, life was rushing on.

She fingered the locket that Sofia had given her long ago on the ship. When she opened the locket, it made the snapping sound that her own heart would make if someone opened it. She took out a small chicken feather, one of dozens that had traveled with Katrina from Lutrek. "You can have only one of them," Katrina had announced imperiously the morning their boat had left New York for the return journey. She'd held the tiniest of the feathers out to Marisia. "I need the rest!"

Probably in Lutrek, right this minute, Katrina's chicken was flapping its way into Grandma's house because Grandma had let down her guard for an instant. The spoiled thing needed only an instant to make its way into a house, as everybody knew. There it would be, puffed up, scratching eagerly under Grandma's table, scooping up crumbs with its yellow beak, its eyes flashing and blinking.

Life went on.

Marisia watched a girl who sat on a crate on the sidewalk so her mother could braid her hair. The girl had a square face and wide nostrils. Her mother ran her fingers through the girl's thick hair and leaned forward to twist it into a heavy plait. The girl, eyes closed, leaned back against her mother. Their bodies joined at the girl's shoulders. Marisia would draw that, she thought. It was a part of all that she again longed to say with her pencils and her paper. She snapped the locket shut, tucked it inside her blouse, and tilted her face into the sun.

CHAPTER TWELVE

WHEN MARISIA ANSWERED THE DOOR, a man towered before her, his mustache as black as the derby hat he wore. If she'd rubbed a genie's lamp, a giant just like this would have popped out, Marisia imagined.

"From Mrs. Heatherston, miss." As he said this, the man tipped his hat and held out a white envelope. Marisia broke the embossed wax seal. "If you are able to attend Mrs. Heatherston's tea, which is to be held in one week, I'm instructed to come for you in the motor car, miss."

Why had Mrs. Heatherston swooped into her life again after two long months without any word at all?

"Miss?"

"Oh—why, tell Mrs. Heatherston . . . tell her I'll come. Thank her for the invitation."

Mrs. Heatherston's smile exposed large teeth and reddened gums. She took Marisia's hand and drew Marisia toward her. In her raspy voice, she said, "Do you know you have a habit of leaning forward just a little when you stand, as if you couldn't wait to join a game that was being played on a field? Anyone with any sense in this room will see that vitality in you, my dear, just the way I did that day in the hat shop. It never hurts to have powerful people take note of you. Remember that." She leaned back, gave Marisia another toothy smile, gripped Marisia's elbow, and moved forward.

Over fans or glasses of champagne or cigars, people inspected Marisia as she circled the room with Mrs. Heatherston. "I want them to see the difference between you and these other girls, like Miss Delamonte here," Mrs. Heatherston said. Pointing a crooked finger, she indicated a young woman who sat nearby.

"Miss Delamonte has no particular ability of any kind, but she's quite decorative in my parlor, don't you think? That guarantees her invitations to many, many parties. Quite decorative, yes. When I was a girl, we wouldn't be able to wear a gown that draped so naturally over the legs like that," Mrs. Heatherston mused, holding a lorgnette up to her right eye. Peering through this eyeglass on its long silver stem, she inspected Miss Delamonte. "No, I'm afraid Miss Delamonte's gown would be thought quite indecent. We wore whalebone hoops and petticoats stiffened with horsehair. No one could tell we had legs at all. Legs were a well-guarded secret."

Miss Delamonte, feeling Mrs. Heatherston's look upon her, glanced up. Her face was very round and her neck very long, so that she made Marisia think of a flower on its stalk.

Mrs. Heatherston went on. "In those days one couldn't breathe, the corsets gripped one so. Girls fainted quite regularly. It was the lungs. The lungs couldn't expand to take in air."

They circled the room again, then stopped before French doors. A man with a head of silver hair, no taller than Marisia herself, waited there, as if he'd been expecting Marisia all along. Abruptly Mrs. Heatherston left Marisia with him. "I must see to other guests, my dear. Mr. Rathbone will take care of you," she said

"The warmth of the day is gone, I'm afraid," Mr. Rathbone said to Marisia and pointed out the glass doors, "or I'd ask you to walk into this garden. Mrs. Heatherston has a taste for things French, and she's brought in French fountains and carved terrace stones and even statues from the castles in that country." He glanced at Marisia. "She told me she's collected you. She collected me years and years ago when I was young."

Marisia smoothed the callused skin of her palms against her skirt. "When she collects people, what does she want to do with them?"

"She simply brings people together. Then she stands back to see what will happen. Mrs. Heatherston is like a scientist mixing up chemicals in a test tube, you might say. You and I, child, we're one of her experiments."

Leaning on a silver-handled cane, Mr. Rathbone stepped away from the windows. Marisia watched him run a hand through his silver hair. His skin was faded, as if a portion of his blood had been drained away. "She told me that you draw quite competently," he said. "Come. She's asked that I show you about. It's quite a museum back here."

On the parquet floors their steps echoed as Marisia and Mr. Rathbone passed through rooms in which pictures covered the walls — pictures of hovering angels and gypsies and horseback warriors and of tables laden with fruit and dead game. Many of the pictures were bigger than Marisia was. She stared up at them in amazement while Mr. Rathbone asked questions. What color would she change  in this painting if she were told to change one? Was the white flower best off where it was on the canvas, or should it be moved? What did she think about the shadow on the man's shirt?

Finally Mr. Rathbone wanted to know which painting Marisia would take home if she could take one and only one. "Show me," he said.

Marisia led Mr. Rathbone to one of the first paintings she'd seen, the portrait of a young man. Light traced the side of his body. It settled in his eyes. Marisia stared at the young man, thinking that if he were alive he'd come down from his wall and march straight out of the house and stride through New York as if the city were his own kingdom.

"Yes," Mr. Rathbone said. "You have a very good eye, child. Mrs. Heatherston's quite right."

Marisia wanted to squirm under his examining look but made herself hold still. Behind Mr. Rathbone on the paneled wall an electric light burned steadily inside its globe of glass. It was nothing like the faltering gas lamp in their own kitchen on Ludlow Street.

Rapping his cane on the floor to draw her attention back to him, Mr. Rathbone announced, "We'll get you into classes. She'll be pleased by that."

"What classes?"

"At Cooper Union." He smiled down at Marisia and shook his head. "The name means nothing to you? I forget that you're a girl living in the tenements. It's a college, a college of art, one of the best in the country and one of the very few that admits women."

"You want me to take art classes in a college? That's what this is all about?"

"Yes," he said. "That's exactly what this is all about. Mrs. Heatherston vouches for your ability. I see for myself that you have a sense of design, a sense of color."

The light on the wall behind Mr. Rathbone looked very, very hot. Marisia felt the heat all across her face. "I can't," she said. "I . . . my brother and I, we have very little money."

"There will be no charge for the classes, no charge to you in any case. There is no cost involved," Mr. Rathbone said.

"But I must work, you see. We send money—my brother and I do—to my parents."

Mr. Rathbone only raised his thin, gray eyebrows and winked one narrow black eye at Marisia. "We'll find ways around any obstacles."

"How?"

"Leave it to Mrs. Heatherston. Money can be provided for your living expenses. There will be at least partial funding, I can assure you." He turned his head. Inside his ear sprouted a sparse tuft of hair. "You have only to concern yourself with developing the talent we think you might have. Prove yourself, child. Leave other considerations to us."

Stepping through a doorway supported by columns, Mr. Rathbone led Marisia back into the large main salon. He rested his cane for a moment on a high table next to some extravagant purple flowers that were imprisoned in a bell jar. Tiredly he rubbed his eyes with both small hands.

Classes, a college! Marisia swept a hand at her straying hair. She brushed one long leg against another. She longed to race straight away from this drowsy little man and from this hushed room with its smells of perfume and orchids and polish. In Ludlow Street people would let her cry out her news to all the world if she wanted, just like the newspaper boy with the cropped yellow hair cried out his headlines when he rushed through the icy, narrow streets.

Across the room, Mrs. Heatherston's head swiveled toward Marisia. Mrs. Heatherston looked at her and then at Mr. Rathbone and then back to Marisia again, waiting for a signal. Excited, Marisia flushed. That seemed to be enough to satisfy Mrs. Heatherston, who nodded firmly, as if concluding a purchase.

"If they need to work for a living, we like students to do something that gives them practice in their studies," Mr. Rathbone told Marisia.

From a shelf, he took down a teacup made of fine china and a plate edged in gold with a floral design on the rim. "They're hand-painted in a shop owned by a Mr. Winemar. The best families in New York buy sets of these pieces, the Astors, the Vanderbilts. You'll go to Mr. Winemar's shop on Hester Street this afternoon and speak with him. He's agreed to use you as an apprentice."

"But I have a job already."

"You'll quit it, then," Mr. Rathbone ordered. "Now, in addition to the salary Mr. Winemar gives you, Mrs. Heatherston will provide you with a financial allotment. That will compensate you for the hours you cannot work, the time you devote to classes at Cooper Union. More specifically, Mr. Winemar will release you on Tuesday and Thursday and Saturday afternoons. You can come to this studio whenever you like, too, even on Sundays. The custodian is always roaming about. Just ring the bell and he comes running."

When Marisia handed the cup back, Mr. Rathbone placed it on the work table. "Another thing," he said, "Mrs. Heatherston wants me to tell you that Miss

Delamonte has taken an interest in you. She's offered you space in her house. It would be an apartment, really—a bedroom and a small parlor."

"Miss Delamonte wants me to live in her house?"

"With her family, a mother and a sister. Her father died three years ago, an accident. A horse threw him. Tragic, really."

Marisia watched Mr. Rathbone tap on the table top between them. The thin, straight fingers were like miniature drum sticks. "It's a Fifth Avenue house," he said. "A true mansion I'm told. You'd have your meals with the family, but otherwise you'd be quite on your own. There you are. It's a step up."

In the light coming through the high windows that circled the room, motes of dust careened this way and that at high speed. "When I was little, I dreamed of living somewhere like that," Marisia said.

"I'll tell Mrs. Heatherston it's all settled, then."

"I don't know if it's settled or not settled." The words jumped out of Marisia's mouth.

Mr. Rathbone's drumming fingers stopped. "Why would you stay where you are? Mrs. Heatherston says you're caged up in that tenement like an animal." His voice was almost angry. His black jacket seemed dangerously shiny, like armor. His small black eyes were like the balls of shot Papa carried in a pouch for his gun. Marisia bit her lip. Why couldn't she think of sensible things? Why couldn't she think of a sensible answer?

"When I look at you, I see your head's spinning. Is that right?" Mr. Rathbone asked.

"Yes," Marisia stammered. "I'm sorry."

"No, no, there is nothing to be sorry about. Miss Heatherston says she's going to stop by next Thursday. You can give her your answer then."

Mr. Rathbone's fingers tapped again. "Remember though that Mrs. Heatherston is expecting you to say yes. In my mind you had better say yes."

"Why would she care where I live?"

"She has a vision of who you'll be after she's all done with you. Mrs. Heatherston's not particularly interested in who you are now, I can tell you. She's interested only in who you will become. You might say that she wants to make you over and then show you off as her very own creation." As he spoke, Mr. Rathbone walked beside the table, tapping his cane like a blind man. At the end of the table he turned to face Marisia. "Do you understand what I'm telling you?"

"If I'm supposed to be her very own creation, then she's the artist. She wants me to pose for her," Marisia said. "I'm to forget everything but the pose she has in mind. She wants me to hold that pose forever, too, like a figure in a painting, her very own painting."

Mr. Rathbone gave a tiny laugh, a laugh that would fit into a teaspoon. "Exactly," he said. "That's exactly right."

Mrs. Clay pulled a sturdy shawl around her short, stout figure. Her red hair bubbled up, framing her white face. "Wasn't I the one who said you were so very, very quick to learn? I thought you might find a way to better your position in time. I've thought on it."

She snapped two fingers together. "Sure if there weren't three other girls in here this very week asking for a position. Decent girls they were, so it's no trouble I'll have in filling your position. But 'tis the pasty-faced ones I'll not abide, with their 'Yes, mum' here and 'Yes, mum' there and that's all you'll be hearing from them all the live-long day. You were not like one of those now, were you? I was thankful for that." She gripped Marisia's hand in hers for a brief instant and then released it. "Off you go, now. I've had a shipment of very pretty Irish linen. 'Tis time I gave it my full attention."

For the last time Marisia left the shop. Already it was growing dark, and ahead of her on the street Marisia saw a man lighting the gas lamps, a flaming pole thrust over his head. She hurried. After the marketing, there would be breakfast dishes to wash because she hadn't

 done them that morning. There was stuffed cabbage to fix for dinner, Marisia reminded herself, and Stefan's torn shirt that needed mending.

At the corner a man yanked on the harness of a horse pulling a load of lumber. Raising his thick fist, he hit the horse a blow on its withers. Marisia darted out and ran past his wagon, and as she did, the man swore at her. She stopped dead in front of him and glared into his face. He stepped back. She stepped forward. He stepped back again, and she stepped forward. From nearby an ice man in his own wagon nearby called out, "You show him, missy." A boy hawking newspapers stopped to stare at her.

Mama would be shocked at her, Marisia thought. Mama would tell her this was no way for a young lady to act in public. Marisia crossed into a circle of light pitched at the ground by a gas lamp and dawdled there, thinking of Mama, staring in front of her. A carriage passed, its driver wrapped in an old quilt, a ragged felt hat pulled down over his forehead. He snapped reins over the horse's rump. "Move it up," he yelled out. His shout roused Marisia from her reverie. Like the horse, she leapt forward.

In the flat Marisia took a shovel full of coal from the scuttle and tossed it into the stove, cracking the door to give the embers air and encourage them to fire. The heat from the stove felt rough on her face, like the nubs on Papa's old jacket did when she rubbed her cheek against it. Marisia shut the door to the stove and swept her hands across her warm face. Then she scratched at the sides and back of her neck with all her fingernails at once, feeling the same pleasure Washington must feel when she did this to him. At Miss Delamonte's if she scratched with all her might, she would have to hide herself away, Marisia knew. There, at all times, she would have to act like a lady.

CHAPTER THIRTEEN

At dinner, waving his fork in the air, Stefan said, "The subways, they'll carry people underground all through the city."

Mr. Pulaski wrinkled his bushy eyebrows. "Running underneath the streets! It's a crazy idea."

"In ten years, two million more people have come into this city—two million of them," Stefan retorted. "There's just no room left above ground. That's the point really. Half the time, traffic can't even budge. Where can we put any more?"

"I won't argue with what you're saying," Mr. Pulaski answered, "but whizzing everybody around underneath the streets...I don't know. Who ever heard of something like that?"

"Where they're building new houses, new apartments, way up there past One hundred fifty-fifth Street, those people can get downtown to work in no time at all. People can live anywhere they want with the subways to ride."

"And why are you smiling about it?" Marisia asked.

When Stefan tapped a spoon on the table, Mr. Pulaski took the spoon from his hand. Lightly he cuffed Stefan on the shoulder. "Go ahead. Tell her now."

"The subway company hired me. I started work today," Stefan said. "I didn't want to say anything until I was sure of the job." His hands clamped against the back of his head, his arms spread into wings, Stefan tilted so far back in his chair that Marisia thought he might fall over. "It's going to be a new world and I'll be building it."

"Unless you go and get yourself fired right off," Mr. Pulaski growled. He looked over to Marisia. "The first day on the job, and he gets to talking with someone who wants him to join the union and start agitating and creating a rumpus."

"If I want to work twelve-hour days and come home exhausted six days a week, fine. I can go it alone. If we want ten-hour days, that'll take unions. I'm right on this, Mr. Pulaski. The bosses aren't going to just give us a ten-hour day because we go and ask nice." More and more, Stefan's rumbling voice reminded Marisia of Papa's voice. If it were Papa talking in Lutrek, Mama would tell Papa he must watch his step and not let anyone hear him saying these things.

It was Mr. Pulaski who played Mama's part. "Others who've talked that way, Stefan, there's been trouble in it for 'em, lots of trouble."

"I know all about it." Stefan stood, cleared dishes from the table, and then began to sing a ballad about a man who loved a girl so much that he howled at the moon night after night until finally he turned into a howling wolf. As children, they'd sung those words with Mama.

In the middle of the ballad, Stefan stopped. "Life isn't any good at all if you don't gamble on making it better," he said to Mr. Pulaski. "A man's got to stand up for himself."

Two hours later Marisia made a trip down the corridor to the toilet where she waited for her turn. The girl who came out was the mother of the baby Marisia could often hear crying through the thin walls of the kitchen. The girl gave Marisia a smile. Barefoot, she shuffled off down the hall like an old person though she couldn't have been more than sixteen or seventeen. Stefan guessed that her husband hit her because sometimes they'd hear her scream and sometimes she had red streaks across her face. In her village someone might have noticed and tried to help, but here in the tenement there was no parish priest or mother or father to speak up for the girl. Marisia had never spoken to her husband, a sad-looking man who always rushed in and out of the building, his eyes looking straight ahead.

Back in her room, Marisia sat on the edge of her bed, curling her toes against the hard edge of the floorboards, stroking her long hair with her fingertips. She was tired, but she didn't want to blow out the candle. If she blew it out, Marisia knew, the room would plunge into a darkness so thick that she couldn't see a finger held close to her face.

She told herself she was too old to be afraid of the dark and then realized it wasn't the dark that made her nervous tonight—not really. It was the thought of the letter she'd sent to Papa that morning, telling him that he and Mama and Adam must come to America and not wait until next year. She and Stefan, Marisia had written, would find an apartment big enough for all of them. It was time, she'd insisted.

Mama would say that she didn't know, that maybe it was too soon, that maybe they should wait, that maybe she wasn't ready to leave Katrina behind in her grave in the little churchyard in Hamburg. But Papa would urge Mama to pack and march her out of the tiny room they'd rented and tell her they must make a new life. They would come.

Marisia could picture how it would be when the family was together again. On nights like tonight Papa would talk politics and Mama would shake her head at him. Papa would tell Stefan to bring him coffee. Stefan would rise to make it, Adam trailing after him, wanting to grind the precious coffee beans. After dinner she and Mama would do dishes, and she would teach Mama some English words. Washington would curl up on a chair close by, his tail flicking, his eyes lazy, his tongue licking at a paw, because he would be there too. Sofia, who kept Washington at her uncle's house where the cat had always lived, would bring him to her.

She had sent the letter. It meant that she wasn't going to Miss Delamonte's. And what would Mrs. Heatherston do when she found out?

Certainly she'd never invite Mama and Papa into her parlor to sit on the stiff chairs with their ornate, carved feet. Of course, Mama and Papa were too ordinary for Mrs. Heatherston's collection of people.

With one long, sturdy finger Marisia traced the rough lines on her palm. They were like firm pencil marks outlining a picture. Next she was on her knees, pulling out real pictures from underneath the bed. From her sewing basket she snatched her pins. With quick movements, Marisia tacked a picture of Katrina onto the wall above her bed.

Next to that she tacked up a picture of a woman hacking the head off a chicken. Marisia pinned up other favorites—her birdlike girl, cross-legged in the dust; a young man with a pick and shovel; a colored woman bending over laundry, her jaw uneven because it had been broken by her master's blow when she was a slave child; the girl with the long braid; a fireman straining to reel out fire hose; her egg-lady; and Mama carrying buckets of water. When all the pictures were pinned to the walls around her, Marisia sat on the bed and looked at them. Then she blew out the candle.

In the pitch-blackness she couldn't see the drawings, but Marisia knew all the people she'd made were still there. She fancied she heard their breathing, a faint whirring sound, like wings plying a pathway through the dark.

On Thursday, as expected, Mrs. Heatherston came to the studio. She held her skirt in her right hand to pull it away from the dirty floor. "Pay no attention to me," she said as she took up a position by the easel where Marisia worked. Her shadow lay on the floor in front of her.

After five minutes Mrs. Heatherston broke the silence with a question. "Have you ever painted on canvas before?"

"No, never," Marisia said. "The oil paints are so slick. Painting with them, it's like skating—like painting on ice. I feel as if I'm always tripping."

"The painting looks like a beginning, but that's not a criticism, my dear. You must always try new things. You must not simply repeat what you can do well."

Just behind Mrs. Heatherston, Mr. Rathbone nodded in agreement. Up and down his head jerked in a motion that irritated Marisia and made her say, "You know, I've thought about your offer, about going to Miss Delamonte's. I want to thank you, but my parents are coming from Hamburg with my younger brother Adam. We want to stay together, all of us."

Mrs. Heatherston stepped forward into a shaft of sun from the high windows and peered at Marisia. In the light, her yellow eyes gleamed. Her head, framed in steel-colored curls, was like the helmet of some Grecian warrior in a book, Marisia thought. Nervously Marisia's hand clenched at her skirt. The material felt thin.

"Consider carefully, my dear, before you give me an answer," Mrs. Heatherston said.

"I have," Marisia answered.

Mrs. Heatherston pinched at a loose fold of skin beneath her chin. It was like the skin on the neck of Katrina's chicken, the dusty bird Mama would sometimes let in the house. What would Miss Heatherston think about letting a chicken into her parlor? What was she saying now in this gravely voice of hers?

"...is an opportunity, one it would be a mistake to pass up. Miss Delamonte is very well placed, my dear." Mrs. Heatherston carried her lorgnette. She waved it. If Marisia believed in such things, she could believe that Mrs. Heatherston was a fairy godmother waving a wand to rescue her. She didn't believe in such things, and again Marisia told Mrs. Heatherston that she would not go to Miss Delamonte's.

Mrs. Heatherston held her head high, looking down upon Marisia. The tendons in her neck twitched like taut ropes. Marisia inspected Mrs. Heatherston as Mrs. Heatherston had always inspected her. What she saw was an ordinary woman, her chest wrapped round in taffeta that was as stiff and brilliant as the shell of a locust. There were flecks in the whites of her eyes like dust, brown spots on the back of her hand, and a beak of a nose, with pinched nostrils. She was as ordinary as the lady with the patch on her eye who sold needles and thread, and there was no need to be afraid of her, Marisia told herself.

Mrs. Heatherston said, "This is a mistake you're making."

"I must make a mistake, then," Marisia answered.

"One is as free to act foolishly as to act wisely, if that's what you want to do," Mrs. Heatherston went on in a voice as rigid as the mound of curls on her head. "There's never been a law against foolishness, which is why so many live so poorly on your street."

Side by side, Marisia and Mr. Rathbone watched the edges of Mrs. Heatherston's skirt stir the dust from the floor into a small cloud as she swept from the room.

Marisia looked at him. "What about the art classes? Will I have to stop coming to classes?"

"Oh, Cooper's Union accepted your application. Your status here no longer depends on Mrs. Heatherston. You are safe enough."

"So she won't make me leave here."

"Mrs. Heatherston won't destroy you. Is that what you thought?"

"I didn't know."

"Well, she won't, but you'll certainly pay a price."

"What price?"

"That remains to be seen. But once, for example, Mrs. Heatherston said to me that some of the illustrated newspapers might be interested in your drawings."

"I've seen those papers."

"Now she'll never introduce you to the editors. It's a lost opportunity."

"Oh, but can't I—"

"Until this moment," Mr. Rathbone interrupted, "you might say the odds were in your favor. Now they're not.

Most fall back if someone like Mrs. Heatherston isn't there to advance them. I've seen it over and over and over again." Mr. Rathbone was backing away from Marisia, his distrustful eyes on her. "Never have I seen anyone look at her the way you did." Abruptly, he turned.

Alone, Marisia faced her canvas and the bright palette of paints. The picture of Papa wasn't working at all, but she'd keep at it until she had it right. With the back of her hand she shoved hair off her face. She brushed Papa's heavy eyelid with light.

Bloodstains blotched the white towel Mr. Pulaski dropped on the kitchen table. Gently he dabbed disinfectant on the cuts around Stefan's eyes. "This one could use stitches or it'll leave a scar. Your third week on that job and it's happened like I said it would if you got mixed up with these unions."

"It's no time for lectures," Stefan retorted. One of his eyes was swollen entirely shut.

"You're sure that you can see? You're not blind?" Marisia heard the anxious pitch of her own voice.

"Yes, Marisia, I can see. You look pale as a ghost. That's what I see."

"I could send for Dr. Heinrich."

"I don't want a doctor."

"He's a friend. He'd come in a minute," she pleaded.

"I don't need a doctor, Marisia. It was worse when the plow horse kicked me three years ago. Remember that?"

Marisia didn't answer the question. Instead she said, "Oh, Stefan, whatever you did, don't do it again."

"Says who? You?" At Stefan's words and his surly tone, Marisia turned her head away and examined a jagged hole at the bottom of the kitchen wall.

"Ignore him, Marisia," Mr. Pulaski said. "It's this head of his. What little sense he had in this head to begin with, they've knocked it straight out of him." Mr. Pulaski slapped Stefan lightly on the cheek. "What she says is reasonable."

"I can't stop. Not after this," Stefan muttered. "I'll be at the next union meeting, do you hear me?" Marisia saw him run his tongue across his split upper lip and tuck his head down, blinking as if he were stopping tears. Bruises covered both sides of his face. A string of wide cuts lined his right cheek. His hair was as dirty and matted as his clothes. It tumbled across his forehead.

When Stefan rose from the kitchen chair, he placed one hand on the back of it to brace himself. He put the other over his ribs, grimacing.

"None of them are broken," Mr. Pulaski said. "I know that for a fact because I checked for broken ribs just now. But bruises you'll have."

"I'm going to bed. I'm going to sleep it off."

Marisia lowered herself into the chair Stefan vacated. "How did it happen?"

"He went out straight after dinner," Mr. Pulaski replied, "the way he usually does, to have his beer at the tavern and see the other lads. Someone must have told whoever wanted to know that Stefan goes there. When he left, they were waiting for him—two men."

"Who are they?"

"A man named Mitchell, Stefan says one of them was called. He didn't know the other."

"Can't he report this to the police?"

"They'll be no help—not when it's union trouble. The bosses see to that," Mr. Pulaski said. "Anyway, it's one man's word against another's because you can be sure nobody saw what happened. Not in that alley they dragged him to."

Marisia made some tea, set the cups out, and poured the steaming liquid into them. "You drink out of the nice one now," Mr. Pulaski told her, taking the chipped cup for himself, his burly fingers closing around its tiny handle. "He'll come around in a day or two. Don't you worry. They meant to teach Stefan a lesson is all, not kill him. Maybe he learned the lesson finally."

"How can you side with them?" Marisia asked angrily.

"I'm not on their side," Mr. Pulaski said, "but Stefan's got to be sensible or he's in for more of the same. That's all."

Blistering sparks ran along Marisia's tongue when she took an angry gulp of her tea. As if set by the fire in her tongue, an idea ignited in her mind. There was the boy at Cooper Union who always wanted to share the food in his black lunch pail with her, whose fingers were always smudged with ink from the printing presses, who was learning the printing trade. He'd told her he could print anything at all—wedding invitations, posters, newspapers, anything.

Posters.

"Are they still there, do you think, those men?"

Mr. Pulaski stared at Marisia. "What are you talking about?"

"Take me to that tavern."

"Why would I do that? Those men must be twice your size and they're not polite, as we both know from looking at your brother's face." Mr. Pulaski blew at his tea, making a whistling noise. "You have as little sense as Stefan if you think you can reason with them."

"I don't intend to reason with them."

"Take you to a tavern? Not tonight, not any night."

"I'll go by myself if you won't go with me."

"You can't go running around the streets at night."

"I have to go there!"

"What good can it possibly do?" Mr. Pulaski leaned forward. The wrinkles in his face were like seams in cloth. Even as they argued, Marisia realized how much she had come to like this homely face.

"Please, Mr. Pulaski," she said. "It's for Stefan."

"No!"

"Please."

She saw the hesitation in his expression as he looked up. He stroked the sleeve of his coat for one long minute to smooth out a crease before he finally said, "You look like an angel singing full blast in heaven when you're about to do things you have no sense doing at all. I must be as crazy as Stefan to even think about going along with you."

"But you will, won't you?"

Quickly, Mr. Pulaski swallowed the rest of his tea and stood. "Get your coat, then. Better do it quick now before I change my mind," he said unhappily.

CHAPTER FOURTEEN

As soon as Mr. Pulaski pushed against the swinging wooden door, Marisia smelled the cigar smoke that drifted from the tavern's dark interior. Mr. Pulaski placed a protective hand on her shoulder. "Whatever your plan is," he said in a low voice, "don't do anything to get us the same bruises Stefan got."

At a table in the back, Mr. Pulaski ordered a whiskey from a man with a thin, waxed mustache. "Her?" the waiter said to Mr. Pulaski, tossing his head in Marisia's direction. He hooked one thumb under his suspenders.

"Nothing for her," Mr. Pulaski replied curtly.

On a bar stool, a woman in a gold dress laughed at what the short man sitting beside her said. The man put his hand around her and picked at her sleeve, just where it met the skin of her shoulder. Mr. Pulaski grumbled, "What I'm doing exposing you to the likes of this company, I don't know."

The waiter returned. On the table he set a short glass

of amber liquid. Mr. Pulaski handed the waiter money and folded his hands on the table in front of him, an eyebrow raised. "Now what?"

Marisia folded her own hands on the table and spoke to the waiter. "A Mr. Mitchell was here earlier. Is he still here?"

"Mitchell, yes, a big spender he is tonight. Shows no sign of leaving any too soon." The man squinted through the smoky room and nodded at the bar. "That's him over there, the biggest one in that lineup sittin' on those bar stools we got, the man in that checkered coat there. See? He don't come in here regular anymore, but I know him from the old days when he did. That was before he wore that diamond pin he's got on. Didn't toss around money like he's doin' tonight—not five or six years ago, he didn't. Just another bloke back then, 'cept bigger than most."

The waiter shifted a plug of tobacco in his mouth, and his left cheek swelled to twice its previous size. "He used to be a fighter back then, and I used to win by bettin' on him. Three, four times I made considerable money."

"The man who's with him, who's that?"

"A Mr. Burnside, I heard him called. I don't know the fellow," the waiter said. Beating a rhythm with his empty tray against his leg, he stamped away.

Marisia said, "There's an empty table by them. Let's sit there."

"Are you crazy?"

Marisia didn't bother to answer Mr. Pulaski's question. Slowly she made her way through the crowded room, past a table where eight or nine men slapped cards down, past an old man slumped drunkenly, his head on his crossed arms, past two young men who grinned at her, past a forlorn middle-aged couple. People in a corner were singing, their song interrupted by regular shouts and bursts of laughter.

Only when she slipped into a seat at the little round table did Marisia look behind her to see if Mr. Pulaski had followed. There he was, disgruntled but faithful, moving between the tables. "I just need one good look at them," Marisia whispered when he settled into the chair by hers, his eyes cast down.

In the mirror that lined the back of the bar Marisia marked every detail in Mitchell's red face. He had loose jowls, a thick upper lip, and an immense nose, which flared at the bottom. His protruding ears had jagged edges, as if mice had nibbled at them. Beside him, sullen and withdrawn, sat Burnside, whose beard was squared off at the sides. His sideburns were graying. His eyes protruded like a frog's. His teeth slanted back, as if someone had pushed them in.

"You've had your look, Marisia. It's enough now. Let's go." Mr. Pulaski stood. He turned into the aisle directly in back of the bar stools. Marisia followed. Her feet stirred the sawdust that lay thick on the floor.

As she came abreast of Mitchell, he spun on his stool. He passed the back of his hand over his heavy mouth, then let it drop like a weight. "Good evenin', girlie."

Marisia couldn't stop herself. She stared into his swamp-colored eyes with all the loathing she felt.

Mitchell bent over until his face was an inch from Marisia's own. "I expect a greeting when I give one," he said. He grabbed her arm.

To the right of his nose was a thick bluish mole. Black hairs grew in his nostrils. "You need a lesson in manners, missy?" Mitchell's fingers pressed together, deliberately stinging Marisia. She wouldn't flinch. He pressed harder, hard enough to raise bruises. She would not flinch, she told herself again.

"Manners, sir? Do not detain a lady against her will, and then perhaps you may speak of manners." Marisia raised her voice. "Let go of my arm! I've never even met you. How dare you lay a hand upon me? I insist you let me go immediately."

A man at a nearby table rose. His companion, a workman with a thick chest, pushed his chair back and scowled. The bartender murmured something to Mitchell. Distracted, Mitchell turned and Marisia wrenched out of his grasp. Her heels clicked on the uneven wooden planks.

The woman in the gold dress gave out a braying donkey laugh as if celebrating Marisia's escape. Glancing back, her hand on the door, Marisia saw Mitchell lurch toward the woman, who snapped her mouth shut and ducked out of his way.

Outside, without saying a word, Mr. Pulaski hustled Marisia to the corner. There he took a turn, and then he turned again, at the next corner, onto a twisting road. Marisia could hear his sharp breathing. Repeatedly, she saw, he glanced behind them. Not for another two blocks did Mr. Pulaski even take his hand off her elbow or speak.

Finally his pace slowed. "Where did you ever learn to talk to somebody like that, the way you did it, like somebody whose got a dozen servants waiting on her day and night?"

"Sofia taught me. She used to make me practice and practice and practice until I wanted to scream. I didn't see the use of any of it, really. Not at the time," Marisia laughed.

"Why did you have to see those two anyway?"

"You'll find out in a few days." A carriage rolled past. Marisia heard the snorting of the gray horse that pulled it. She could smell the beast. The pungent odor made her think of the barn in Lutrek, where she would sometimes nap near their horse's stall on hot afternoons when she wanted to hide from Mama and the errands Mama would ask her to run. In that safe childhood world, pigeons skittered in the rafters and spiders worked webs and mice nosed along walls.

"Come on," Mr. Pulaski said, pulling her away from her memories of that refuge. "You almost got us killed. It's enough for one night."

He tucked the collar of his coat around his neck. The light from the street lamp vibrated on the sidewalks as they hurried toward home.

"Yes, I can print 'em up." Paul's smile cut straight across his narrow, freckled face. He drew a finger across Marisia's drawings and the letters that Marisia had copied so carefully, making them look exactly like the letters she'd seen on the posters in the post office or on the sides of fences and buildings. WANTED, the letters said.

"Assault and battery and attempted murder. It's not a lie. It's what they did to Stefan," she told Paul.

"Your brother, he's not the first these two blokes done that to either. Believe me. That type is paid regular to beat people 'til they can't see straight. Me and my mates, we've 'ad no end of trouble with that sort. We'll spread these posters far and wide for you when I get 'em all printed up. Where'd you come up with that idea? In English it's what we call ingenious. That's what it is." Marisia stared at Paul's thin, knifelike mouth, trying to understand the words that poured out. One of his eyes was slightly crossed, giving him a madcap appearance, and both were such a light blue they were almost clear.

Paul went on. "It's the kind of trick I've always liked. I wouldn't 'ave expected it of a girl. And for art, it's not bad for a girl, either. You've got a good hand at it, like," he said, eyeing Marisia's work. "It's the real thing you got here. You could go into the business. 'Course, we wouldn't dare use these here as samples now to find you a job doin' that, would we? Wouldn't want to let the cat out of the bag."

Marisia wondered what a cat and a bag had to do with it.

"No, anybody asks, me and my mates'll keep your name out of it. We'll make sure nobody ever figures out

it was you behind this caper. You're worth protectin',
you are!"

"Look at this," Mr. Pulaski whooped, barging through
the door into the kitchen. At the sink Marisia turned.

Stefan stared as Mr. Pulaski slapped two posters
down on the table. "It's the men who got me in the alley,"
Stefan said. "What is this?"

"Look what she did!" Mr. Pulaski shouted while
Marisia grinned at him. "They tell me people are stopping these two in the streets. If they say they didn't do
anything, nobody believes them. They get hustled off
to the police. When the police straighten it all out
finally, they're let go, but then someone else is wanting
to turn them in at some other station to collect on the
reward."

Stefan stared at Mr. Pulaski. "What are you talking
about?"

"These posters are Marisia's drawing, I'm telling you."

"You did these?" Stefan asked, tilting his head to look
at Marisia. "You? I didn't know you could..." Stefan's
voice trailed off as he sat down, flicking at Burnside's
mouth with his finger. "They're good."

Her hand on the back of the kitchen chair, Marisia
picked aimlessly at peeling splinters of wood with her fingernail. Stefan said her drawings were good. They were
professional, Paul claimed. The real thing, he'd said.

No longer hearing Mr. Pulaski's voice, Marisia stared
at the tabletop.

Mr. Rathbone had once mentioned the illustrated

papers, saying that Mrs. Heatherston would no longer introduce her to the editors because she hadn't done what Mrs. Heatherston wanted. After that, Marisia had bought several copies. In those she'd seen pictures of fires and of trials in the courts...

Everybody in New York was talking about how the subways were about to change the city completely. For the readers of the papers it was a fairy-tale story of high-speed cars that could race under the streets and carry thousands. What if there was another story to be told in pictures alongside that fanciful one? The real story of the people...the people who..."Stefan, can you take me to where you work?"

Stefan rubbed his hand over the wild cowlick that reared up on his head. "Why? What for?"

"Don't ask her what for, boy," Mr. Pulaski shouted. "She's got some other plan now in that head of hers. Tell her yes."

"You can't take her down there," the man in charge told Stefan firmly. He pulled his brimmed cap down to straighten it. "Never was a woman down there, never will be," he said.

Marisia stepped forward. "It's a job, you see. The *New York Herald* needs illustrations for an article on the subways that they'll be running in two weeks."

She held out her sketchpad. "Next week they'll be sending out the reporters, but I need to get the pictures drawn first. They'll want to talk to you, to you and other men in charge here who know exactly what's going on. You'll find your name in the newspaper soon enough. I'll make sure you get some free copies if you like."

Marisia put the point of her pencil on the paper. "If you would spell your name out for me so we have it correctly, sir," she said in a businesslike voice.

The man in the wide-brimmed cap shifted his weight  to his left leg and stuck his hand in his pocket. Letter by letter he spelled out his name, peering at Marisia's pad while she wrote. Workers standing by him studied Marisia as if she were an odd specimen that had dropped in front of them from out of the sky.

Hitching up his trousers, the man in the cap said, "Better spell it back now to make sure they get it right." After she had, he shook his head at her in disbelief. "This way, then. All's I can tell you is watch your step. I'm not responsible for any girl breaking her neck down there."

Stefan led Marisia down a rickety staircase into the world that ran below the street. "What kind of tale were you telling him?"

"It won't be a tale. It's going to be the truth. You'll see," Marisia said.

"How are you going to get this newspaper story of

yours, then? Who are you to do something like that, Marisia?"

Coughing, she waved her hand at the dusty air. "People want to know about this. I know they do."

Stefan took off his jacket. "Maybe they do after all. Awful, isn't it? You'll see. At the end of the day you're not going to get the taste of dust out of your mouth, no matter how much you drink to chase it away."

Squatting, her sketchpad braced against her knees, Marisia ran her pencil along the smooth pages, trying to catch the hard crook in an old man's shoulder or the frown on a young man's upturned face. Covered with sweat, her fingers slipped and the lines on her paper staggered.

It didn't matter. It was as if she were mining in this dark subterranean world, Marisia mused. In the few hours she had, she must pull out the ore as quickly as she could. Later, when she brought these rough drawings to the surface, there'd be time to clean them and polish them until anyone could see in these men all that she saw herself, the traces of gold in ordinary rock.

CHAPTER FIFTEEN

THE ELEVATED COLUMNS CAST THIN, towering shadows across the cobblestones. The black mare trotted in and out of them, her hooves sounding out a staccato beat. Inside the carriage, Marisia sat upright and tense. "This time nothing's going to go wrong," she said aloud in defiance of her silent worry that in fact things might.

Dr. Heinrich said, "This city will be like another world for your mother and father. It'll be a real shock. You'd better expect that, you know."

"But we're here." Stefan pulled his socks up and tilted his polished shoes to inspect them. "We'll help."

"Everything's turned around," Marisia said. "I'll have to teach Mama about the money and tell her how to shop. We'll show Papa how to go about getting a job. It's strange, as if they're the children."

Dr. Heinrich twined his fingers together. "Don't tell them that! It will be hard enough for your parents as it is."

Stefan sat straight on the seat, slouched, then straightened again. He crossed and uncrossed his legs. He was fretting, too. With the palms of both hands, he slicked his hair back against the sides of his head. Two girls on a corner stared through the window at him. One giggled and batted flirty, dark eyes, but Stefan didn't notice.

The carriage moved ahead. Three boys ran alongside it, hands out to beg for money. Silently Marisia asked her what Mama would think of those bold American girls on the corner or these ragged boys. Aloud, Marisia said, "Mama will be the most homesick of all of us. She'll miss the wildflowers and the trees."

"One day, we'll take her to Bronx Park on the train if you like," Dr. Heinrich replied. "Last year, I picked berries out there with some friends of mine. It's a regular woods, a forest—trees, birds, grass, fresh air, sunshine, all of it. It'll be for your mother like a bit of Poland, a place where she'll feel at ease."

Removing his glasses, Dr. Heinrich twirled them for a moment. "Some can't ever get used to life here. America's not what they expected. I've seen some people, patients of mine, who become angry about that. In the end, their anger does them in. They are so furious at the loss of their dreams that they simply can't get on with real life."

"Father's like that," Sofia said.

"He's one I was thinking about," Dr. Heinrich said gently. He watched Sofia's face, as if he wanted to say more but couldn't. She looked back at him. Hair fell across her scarred cheek. Sofia pushed it away.

"Sooner or later," Stefan said, "Mama and Papa will get used to everything. It will just take time." When he leaned forward, the jacket he wore was tight across his back because in the past months his shoulders had broadened. Marisia thought he looked like a plank of timber stuffed into human clothes. "I'll take Adam to the moving pictures on Sunday," he said.

"The problem is," Marisia said, "Adam's going to like New York too much. He'll want to play baseball, and collect those baseball cards they make, and swim off the piers in the East River. Mama will have a hard time keeping him at home."

Dr. Heinrich said something else. Stefan answered back. They began talking about American farming methods and acreage in New Jersey.

Impatiently Marisia waited for them to finish the conversation. She wanted to tell Dr. Heinrich about her interview with a newspaper editor only yesterday. In two of the newspaper offices she had visited, no one would look at her work or bother with her at all. But in the third office, she was asked to talk with a junior editor. He had sat at a cluttered desk and looked at Marisia through the thick glasses he wore. Between thumb and pointer finger he held a cigar, and he had punctuated his sentences by puffing at it or jabbing it in the air.

Yes, the man had said to Marisia, he would look at her drawings of the men building the subway, and, yes, he'd consider a story. Marisia must contact him in five or six days, he'd said, to learn of his decision.

Facing this man, Marisia had pretended to know

everything about publishing her pictures when in fact she didn't know anything at all. Stefan had laughed when she had told him about the meeting. Mr. Pulaski had cheered her on. But neither of them had any idea how one conducted the business.

Could Dr. Heinrich tell her? Did he know somebody who could? Now he and Stefan were talking about American apple varieties and methods of cultivation. Restlessly, Marisia brushed the toe of her shoe over the floorboards. She looked out of the carriage and imagined the newspaper editor in his smoky room. She imagined herself at their next meeting, telling him that he must accept her pictures. He must!

And if he didn't?

If he didn't, then she would show her illustrations to every newspaper man in every newspaper office on Park Row. She would attend art classes at Cooper Union, too, in spite of the fact that Mrs. Heatherston had withdrawn financial support for living expenses. And she would work for Mr. Winemar, who had told her that she was to begin her apprenticeship by painting in the designs others drew on his fine china.

"It is a beginning," Mr. Winemar had said.

A beginning.

She did not know what the ending would be, not yet. All that she did know was that she would continue to paint and draw. By now she knew that she *must* paint and draw.

Overhead, an elevated train passed. The horse shied. The carriage pitched sideways. Marisia returned to the here-and-now. She glanced at Sofia and took Sofia's hand in her own. Sofia leaned her head next to Marisia's and said something.

"What?"

Sofia pressed her lips right against Marisia's ear and said it again. The train passed on. The carriage righted itself.

Dr. Heinrich's voice went on as if nothing had changed when everything had. "You are so good for Sofia," Marisia blurted out. "I'm so glad you're going to be married!"

For a moment Dr. Heinrich looked startled. Then he nodded his agreement and gave Marisia his long, boyish smile. Behind his gold-rimmed glasses his eyes were kind and eager. His eyes were just right.

At Ellis Island Stefan and Marisia left Dr. Heinrich and Sofia on a bench and pushed into the crowd by the ferry landing, where they'd told Papa and Mama they would wait. On the other side of the wire fence was the large brick building with its turrets and its air of importance. Marisia could clearly imagine the pandemonium inside, the milling and confusion, the high-ceilinged rooms echoing with voices, the lines of people winding past inspection points, and the families, whose children huddled together in bewilderment—she remembered it all.

Marisia tried to circle around a bulky woman who blocked her view. She couldn't. She was wedged in. "Can you see anything?" she asked Stefan.

"People are coming out, but I don't see Papa or anyone. They must still be in there." Three people, shouting names, holding hands, surged to the left, their faces expectant. Quickly Marisia moved into the space that opened up. She put one outstretched hand on the fence to claim the spot. For over an hour she and Stefan waited there, sometimes leaning their faces against the cool wire.

"I'm hungry," Stefan said. Marisia took a loaf of bread from her bundle and broke off a long piece of it for him. She broke off a piece for herself. She ate without tasting the food.

The sun tipped from the center of the sky into the west. A wind stirred the water into choppy waves. From time to time people filed out of the giant, dark building, but it was always someone else's father or mother or son or daughter or grandfather or fiancée or brother who had come into America.

Papa had a large cloth bag over his right shoulder and another over his left. He was bent under their weight, but again and again his head bobbed up as he looked for them. Mama carried a big straw suitcase, holding it in front of her with both hands. When the black babushka

Mama wore around her head slipped down, she stopped to tighten it. By Mama's side, his face turned up to hers, Adam was saying something. Adam had grown, Marisia noticed. His head came to Mama's shoulder. As she watched him, Marisia's hand tightened on the locket at her throat. She shouted his name and then Mama's, but her calls were drowned out by the shuffling noises of the wind and of the people all around her.

Nearer they came, and nearer. Stefan flapped both arms above his head, as if he were a giant bird getting ready to take off into the sky, and it was then Papa finally saw them. Pointing, shouting, he turned toward Mama. At that, Mama's head tilted toward them too. Papa's steps quickened. He passed through the gate. In front of Stefan and Marisia, he dropped his bundles onto the ground and threw an arm around her. "Papa," Marisia murmured. "Papa." He bent over Marisia, sheltering her from the gusts of wind coming off the ocean. She ran her hand up and down his arm. The fabric of his jacket was rough against her palm, and so familiar it made Marisia want to cry out.

Mama arrived. She pulled Marisia against her. Marisia heard Mama's hasty breathing and her own, like an echo. Over Mama's shoulder, Marisia could see the sun. It hung in a reddening, western sky. It was so big, it looked as if it would burst wide open. It was a fairy-tale sun, full of promise.

Adam was telling Stefan about something that had happened on the boat, about a sailor who had taken him up into the rigging. Papa put a hand on the back of

Adam's neck and then stuck the other hand in the pocket of his jacket. Marisia had seen Papa in a pose like this a hundred times, she thought.

"Why am I crying when I'm happy? Somebody tell me that!" Mama said, releasing Marisia from her embrace.

Marisia stared past Mama at the descending sun, which cast a blazing strip of light across the water. That bright band was as broad as one of New York's great streets, Marisia saw, and as shiny as gold.

There, out on the water where she never would have thought to look for it, was one of the streets of gold that Elsa had told Marisia she would find. That street of gold would disappear when day ended, but it would reappear, too. While Adam rattled on at Stefan in his piping voice, Marisia squinted straight at the water and into the wild, clamorous light. For now, Marisia told herself, she was ready to believe in streets of gold. She was ready to believe any fantastic, incredible story that the sun had to tell.

About the Author

 Marie Raphael is a life-long educator who has worked with young people at many levels and in many situations—from a Harlem pre-school in New York City to college classrooms in Boston and California to a rural junior high school. Presently, she lives in northern California and supervises student teachers at Humboldt State University. *Streets of Gold* is her first novel.